OWL BERRY MYSTERIOUS

OWL STAR WITCH MYSTERIES BOOK 12

LEANNE LEEDS

Owl Berry Mysterious
ISBN: 978-1-950505-81-4
Published by Badchen Publishing
14125 W State Highway 29
Suite B-203 119
Liberty Hill, TX 78642 USA

For permissions contact: info@badchenpublishing.com

CONTENTS

OWL BERRY MYSTERIOUS

CHAPTER ONE

$\mathcal{A}$ll of us had somehow ended up at the charming berry farm, situated on the town's outskirts, for reasons that remained a puzzle to me.

The air was thick with the smell of ripening fruit as Eddie walked beside Emma, who pushed a carriage. "Why did we come here again, Emma? It's a strawberry farm, but it's not strawberry season," he said, eyeing her cautiously.

Emma ignored Eddie's question and continued to look around, taking in the lush fat blackberries that shimmered with blue and purple hues in the sun's rays. She breathed deeply, savoring the fragrant aroma that filled the air. "Isn't it wonderful?" she asked no one in particular. "I remember that scent from when I was a child."

My sister Ayla and her boyfriend Mel strolled along, their arms intertwined as they gazed at each other with tender fondness. It was an idyllic moment of serenity and joy, with a mellow warmth of contentment enveloping them.

It practically made my skin itch.

It seemed crazy that giving birth to a half-human, half-werewolf baby could profoundly affect Emma's personality, but it had. My closest non-family companion had changed from a brave small town investigator to a maternal divinity, mastering the art of diaper changing with the same deadly precision she once used to bring down criminals.

"If there are blackberries here and not strawberries," Lothian asked, his eyebrow arching with suspicion, "why call it Strawberry Fields Farms?"

"You know, I just noticed something." Ayla stopped walking and turned around. "Do you always sound like you're interrogating someone?"

"Yes," he said, crossing his arms with guarded curiosity. A faint smile played on his lips as he listened for answers.

"Florida grows winter strawberries," I

explained, pointing toward the rows of strawberry plants. "You can still get some u-pick strawberries in April, but it's starting to taper off by then." I turned in the other direction and pointed to the blackberry hedgerows. "That's what's ripe right now. You can also get raspberries, squash, sweet corn, tomatoes, and if you look over there." I pointed to a far-off patch of land. "I think there's a small watermelon patch. They're just coming into season."

"They grow more strawberries than anything else," Emma added. "It's just not the season for it."

"How do you know so much about crops in Florida?" the werewolf asked me.

"I'm a witch," I told him. "Maybe not the most impressive one my mother ever raised, but I know some stuff."

"We're here," Emma answered Eddie's question from a few moments ago, "because my family used to come here during berry season when I was a child, and it's where I have some of my best memories. Barry Fields, the owner, always remembered my name and pretended that there was a special berry bush just for me and my brother Rex. It was like the berries were grown just for us." Emma moved around to the front of the carriage, carefully cradling the baby's head and back with her expert touch. She cooed softly, her voice a soothing melody, as she held the infant close to her chest. "I wanted to share it with him."

"You know he won't remember this trip," I told her. "Babies don't have long-term memories that—"

"Hey, Astra?"

"Yep?"

"Shut up."

Hunter Renzo was an adorable baby.

Even I—who was not particularly fond of babies—had to admit that.

He had a tiny face creased with soft wrinkles, his cheeks were rosy, and his eyes were bright and unnaturally curious for a two-month-old baby. His small mouth made soft gurgling noises as if he was answering the words of comfort that his mother whispered to him.

"I was expecting this to be more like Knott's Berry Farm and less like...this," Lothian said, gesturing around at the happy children playing in the berry fields and people walking with berry baskets. "There are no roller coasters. I was hoping for roller coasters."

"You thought I would bring my tiny newborn

baby to a place with roller coasters?" Emma growled, her frigid tone full of outrage.

"No, ma'am, he did not," Eddie said, jumping in. "He was making a joke."

Lothian nodded, his brow knitted with doubt. "Yes. A joke."

"It's the chimera cells," my sister Althea told me a few days ago. "They make her a little wolf-like now."

The chimera, according to Greek mythology, was a monstrous fire-breathing hybrid creature composed of different animal parts. Humans called them microchimeric cells, tiny fragments of a baby's cells that can stay in a mother's bloodstream for years after birth. Human pregnancy, werewolf pregnancy, made no difference—Emma likely got some werewolf cells through that same process.

I didn't need a scientist to tell me that's probably why she periodically growls now.

Emma inhaled sharply, her nostrils flaring. "I don't think I'm wrong to expect more respect from you, Lothian."

The werewolf stood in a defensive stance, his hands held halfheartedly up in submission. Lothian's usually fierce eyes were softened with remorse. "You're absolutely right," he said, his voice gentle. "Forgive me."

We stood there for a moment, the tension in the air wafting away slowly like the warm breeze that rustled the leaves of the berry bushes.

Finally, Emma smiled and said, "Cool. Let's go pick some berries."

* * *

WE SPENT the next few hours of the relaxing morning picking berries, and it was the most peaceful I had felt in a while.

Emma and Eddie walked ahead, their laughter ringing like music as the baby cooed at me over Emma's shoulder, his tiny fists curling up against his cheeks. I marveled at how Emma handled the baby, her movements graceful and deliberate as if she had been a mother for years.

Ayla and Mel were close behind, and I couldn't help but smile. They were deep in conversation, their heads bent close together as they whispered secrets back and forth. Seeing my sisters finally breaking free from the strict rules our mother had always tried to impose on us was a heartening sight. She was finally fully embracing her path, and I couldn't be happier for her.

Lothian and I walked in comfortable silence, our steps matching each other's effortlessly, even though we didn't exchange words.

The day was perfect.

"Emma!" a man I didn't recognize called out. He was tall and broad-shouldered, with skin tanned a deep brown from years spent toiling under the sun. He wore a faded denim overall and a beat-up straw hat, and his kind face was framed by a salt-and-pepper beard. "Emma Sullivan! Is that a baby in your arms? A new brother? One of your friends' babies? You're not old enough to have one of your own, right?"

"Mr. Fields!" Emma called out. Her face lit up as she hurried toward him. "It's so good to see you again. How have you been?"

The man laughed and hugged Emma tightly. "I'm doing well, Emma. Thank you for asking. And who is this little one?"

"This is Hunter," Emma said, her voice full of pride. "He's my son."

Mr. Fields' face softened. "Well, it's my pleasure to meet you, young Hunter. Welcome to the farm." He paused, his eyes twinkling as he spoke. "Maybe one day you and your family can return, and we'll have a special berry bush just for you."

The baby giggled.

"Now, I apologize for calling you Emma Sullivan," Mr. Fields said with a gallant bow. "What's your name now?" He glanced at Eddie and then at Lothian. "And which one of these strapping young men is your husband? Surely the baby's father made an honest woman of you?"

I gritted my teeth.

When is a question not really a question?

When asked in the south, the asker is already sure of the answer.

But doesn't like it.

Mr. Fields spoke in a soft, dignified southern drawl that made it clear he was far from pleased at the unmarried mother status of Emma. Heck, the entire town of Forkbridge had buzzed with the scandal of Eddie and Emma's non-wedding, and I highly doubted that news had missed the Strawberry Fields Farm.

Which, to be fair, was Emma's fault.

That everyone was talking about it, I mean.

In a desperate attempt to "make an honest woman" of Emma, Eddie had pulled out all the stops; he had arranged an opulent proposal at the fanciest seafood place on Main Street, hired a band to play their favorite song, and got down on one knee with a diamond that sparkled like a disco ball in the candlelight.

The moment he got down on one knee, she pushed herself up from the table, waddled over to him, and doused him and his grand gesture with an entire bottle of Pellegrino. That kind of scene gets talked about in a small town. Especially when the town's teens posted a video of it online.

I didn't feel bad for Eddie.

I'd warned him.

"I assure you, I am still an honest woman regardless of my marital status, but no, I did not marry and am not married, Mr. Fields," Emma told him pleasantly. "I do have a family, though." She gestured to Eddie, Lothian, Ayla, Mel, and me. "And Hunter will have plenty of family to love him. This strapping middle-aged man—"

"Ouch," Eddie said.

"—is Hunter's father, Eddie."

"It's a pleasure to meet you, sir," he said, extending his hand toward the older man. "I can assure you that Hunter will be well taken care of."

I rolled my eyes.

And people wondered why small towns were hotbeds of people being in everyone's business.

Mr. Fields smiled and shook Eddie's hand.

"That's good to hear, son. You've got yourself a solid woman to be the mother to your son. I wish you luck in taming her." He clapped his hands together. "Speaking of taming wild women, have you seen Scarlett, Emma? She's working over by the jam stand."

I clenched my jaw so tightly that my teeth threatened to splinter.

"You okay?" Lothian snickered, his eyes glinting with mischief.

I swallowed my annoyance and silently endured.

"You look a little tense there, Astra," Lothian purred, his smirk oozing that mocking superiority that made me want to punch him in the face.

"Shut up, Lothian."

After Mr. Fields left, Emma turned to us with a determined look in her eye. "I want to go see Scarlett. I haven't seen her in a while. Last time was when we bumped into each other at the diner, and that was two, three years ago?"

Eddie nodded. "None of us know the way to the jam stand. Lead on, my love."

Emma led us through the little paths of the farm and eventually through a large, open barn. The old wooden structure contained a sprawling marketplace. The place was teeming with people, all bustling about as they browsed the colorful stalls filled with fresh produce, handmade goods, and more. "Is this an actual Farmers' Market?"

Emma nodded. "Isn't it awesome?"

"How did I not know about this?"

"Because your diet is horrible, and your mother never shopped here."

There was a pleasant atmosphere of friendly competition among the farmers as they tried to entice buyers to purchase their goods. I saw vendors helping customers, displaying their wares, and chatting amiably about their products everywhere I looked. Meanwhile, children ran around, playing games and laughing as they explored the market.

"Why don't we have a booth here?" I asked, glancing at a woman selling bath salts and handmade lotions.

"Because the Farmers' Market organization wouldn't allow you guys to have a booth here," a woman said as she stepped out from behind a booth. She stood tall and proud, her black clothes clinging to her figure and emphasizing her curves.

"I'm sorry?" I asked.

"Yep, your mom tried. It was a no-go." Her arms

were adorned with intricate tattoos that glimmered in the light, and there was an air of confidence about her, a sense that she was in control of her own destiny and unafraid to take on the world. "They're against witches. I don't think they'd even let me in the barn if my family didn't own the place."

* * *

"Scarlett!" Emma ran toward the woman and enveloped her in a hug. "It's so good to see you."

"I guess this is the jam lady," Lothian said.

"Can you talk without being snarky?" Ayla asked.

He cocked his head. "Why would I want to?"

Scarlett returned Emma's hug with a squeeze and laughed. "You haven't changed a bit, Em. Still the wild and free spirit I remember considering the company you're keeping, huh?"

My eyes narrowed.

How did this woman know that Emma was hanging around with two werewolves, two witches, and a...gas station attendant?

Okay, granted, she probably wasn't talking about Mel Platt.

We stood by as the two friends quickly caught

up, swapping stories of the past few years and reminiscing about old times when they played together as children. Eventually, they focused their attention on us.

"So this is your family?" Scarlett asked, her eyes twinkling with mischief.

Emma nodded. "This is Eddie, my son's father." She pointed to me. "This is Astra, a close friend of mine. And these two youngsters—"

"Can vote in less than two years, so we're not youngsters," Ayla finished and then extended her hand. "Ayla Arden. This is my boyfriend, Mel Platt. I think we've met before—I've seen you in my family shop."

"Yes! Yes, that's right." Scarlett smiled. "It's nice to meet all of you. I'm so happy your family could make it to the farm." Her eyes brightened as she glanced at Hunter, and she reached out, ruffling his hair. He smiled. "And this must be Hunter. I've heard quite a bit about him." She extended her arms and made a motion. "May I?"

Lothian's every muscle went rigid.

"Down, boy," I whispered calmly.

Emma agreed and held out the baby. Scarlett cradled the tiny form and nuzzled his small cheek. "He's so precious. You're going to be such a great mom. What are you most looking forward to, do you think?"

"Thanks," Emma said, her voice full of love for her son. "Honestly, I can't wait to take him out shooting for the first time." Scarlett held Hunter out to Emma, who gently took her son back into her arms. Hunter wrinkled his nose and let out a soft huff, then settled into Emma's arms and fell asleep. "How are things here?"

Scarlett's face fell, and she looked sad. "Ah, it's been a bit tense at home lately," she said, quiet but determined. "My father...he disapproves of my not being married. He thinks I should have settled down by now. Which, you know, if it was just an opinion, I could handle it, but...he had a health scare last year," she admitted, lowering her voice. "It made him reevaluate leaving me the farm. He thinks there should be a man in charge."

Ayla and Mel exchanged glances.

Emma nodded in understanding and placed a comforting hand on Scarlett's shoulder. "That must be really hard," she said gently.

"Do you have a younger brother he's going to leave it to instead?" I asked.

"I'm his only child. Unless he leaves it to Brock Taylor, there is no one else." Scarlett pointed to a man in his midthirties, his hands clasped behind his back as he looked over the market with an aura of authority. His tall, muscular frame and sun-kissed skin suggested a life spent working outdoors, while his cropped, light brown hair and strong jawline exuded rugged charm. "Brock's worked here for ten years, and he's a huge help to my dad and all, but I can do anything he can do."

"That's not fair!" Ayla said, her voice full of indignation. "That's completely sexist. Your father is a misogynist!

"Yes. This isn't right, and it's not fair," Scarlett declared, her voice rising with passion. "But this is the way things are. I will not accept defeat—I will fight for what is mine, and no one will take it away from me."

I wished Scarlett hadn't said that quite as loud as she did.

CHAPTER TWO

The following day, I awoke to the sound of glasses clinking and the smell of fresh-baked bread wafting through the air. I stretched my arms and sat up, blinking away the fog of sleep. Sunlight shone through the open bay window, and I could hear the distant murmur of voices from down below.

"Time to get up," I muttered, throwing off my covers and sliding out of bed.

"You think?" Archie asked sarcastically from his perch in the window. "You know, it's your turn to run Spellbound Emporium today with Ayla."

"What time is it?"

"Almost nine in the morning."

"We don't open until ten. Relax."

Spellbound Emporium was the new name of the magic shop my sisters and I inherited from my mom when she passed. It had been called Athena's Garden, but we'd decided to disassociate the shop from any Greek god. We wanted people to know that the store was open to all, no matter their religion or background or god, and this was no longer Athena's temple. Yes, I still had Archie and the star power, but despite that, the goddess hadn't roped us into saving anyone in quite a while.

I quickly showered, changed into jeans and a t-shirt, grabbed my favorite leather boots, and headed downstairs. Ayla and Althea were already in the kitchen, drinking coffee and chatting.

"Good morning," I said, yawning.

"Rise and shine," Ayla said, pouring me coffee.

"I rose," I told her, sitting at the table and grabbing a piece of toast. "It will take me a little bit to shine this morning. What's on the agenda today?"

"We've got a shipment of crystals coming in," Althea said. "We need to get them unpacked, sorted, and priced. We also need to restock the shelves and clean up the store."

"And by we, you mean Astra and me," Ayla

said with a hint of sarcasm. "You hate sorting and pricing crystals. Somehow, whenever you order them, they only arrive on days you're not working." She snatched two pieces of bacon, popping one on her plate and tossing the other toward her loyal hound Cerberus. "It's amazing how well that works out for you."

"So do the ordering."

"I hate ordering."

"Then it all works out," I said, reaching for the morning paper Aunt Gwennie had set on the kitchen table, but I couldn't quite get it. "Can I have that? No one else wants to read it first?" I asked, looking around at my sisters, who simply shrugged.

"None of you read the paper?" I asked.

Ayla made a face. "If anything important happens, my phone will tell me," she said dismissively.

Aunt Gwennie grabbed the paper and handed it to me. "So, how did you girls do yesterday at the farm?" she asked, changing the subject.

"It was great!" Ayla replied. "We picked a bunch of berries and then went shopping at the Farmers' Market."

I smiled, but as I unfolded the newspaper, my eyes were drawn to the front page headline:

"Local Strawberry Farmer Dead. Farmer's Daughter Arrested." On the front page was a picture of a smiling Barry Fields. I scanned the article quickly, but it did not mention how he died or when, only that his body was found early yesterday evening in his blackberry fields.

Stunned, I glanced up at my sisters and aunt. "Did you guys see this?" I turned the paper around and held it up like a piece of damning evidence in a courtroom.

Althea gasped, her breath catching in her throat. "Oh my gods," she murmured. "That's awful. You guys were just there yesterday."

Ayla nodded solemnly, her face pale with shock. "We talked to Scarlett," she whispered. "She remembered me from the magic shop. She shops at the Emporium sometimes."

"What are we going to do?" Ami asked quietly.

I looked down at the paper, a lump in my throat as I remembered Barry Fields, who had been so warm and friendly to us the day before, albeit sexist and misogynistic, now gone forever, and his daughter in police custody. I didn't know them well, but I could tell Emma would be heartbroken. "Why would we do anything?" I inquired.

"It's a feeling I have. Like a weird tug or a

pull," Ami said as she pulled out a deck of tarot cards from her pocket. "I think we're supposed to help her."

"What do you mean, Ami?" Aunt Gwennie asked.

"Just what I said. I can't explain more than that."

Ayla and I exchanged surprised glances, and she shrugged as I turned back to Ami. "Look, I'm not trying to roll my eyes at your instincts or anything, but none of those cards are glowing, no gods have intervened to demand we spring to action, and no ghosts—" I looked at Ayla, and she shook her head. "—have shown up here asking for our help. From my perspective, we should avoid it and let the police handle it."

Althea nodded slightly at me. "I agree with Astra."

"I don't." Ami's hands moved quickly and confidently as she expertly shuffled the deck of cards. "We need insight," she said solemnly. "Let us see what the cards say about our situation." She laid the cards out in a perfect circle before her, with the four of us looking on.

I narrowed my eyes, feeling skeptical.

Now, I want to be clear—I trusted my sister.

Heck, all of my sisters.

But I couldn't help but wonder if interpreting the cards with a personal stake in the outcome, or a desire to see it go one way or the other, would affect the interpretation.

Just saying.

One by one, she flipped the top card onto the table. The cards seemed to have an almost magnetic pull, and Ami gazed at them with intensity as if expecting them to have the answers she sought. She spoke solemnly, asking for insight into the situation.

Finally, she looked up.

"The cards tell us that Scarlett did not kill her father," she said grimly. "Now, I don't know about any of you, but I can't let someone just go away to prison for a murder they didn't commit. Can you?"

* * *

"WHEN THEY SAY US, they really mean me. I know Ami's trying to find herself after Mom died, and I get that, but she's not Nancy Drew." I slipped out of my everyday clothes and put on my special bulletproof outfit: a pair of black cargo pants and a black t-shirt (thanks to Althea's modification of my old military uniform) with a lightweight, dark-gray vest. The fabric was tightly woven, magically enhanced, and as strong as Kevlar.

"We're all in this together," Archie said with a determined glint in his eye. "It can't always be you at the head of the sister brigade leading the charge into whatever war or fight or murder you're leading them into."

"Who's side are you on here?"

"Mine. You haven't figured that out yet?"

I rolled my eyes at my owl's typical self-involved bravado. I looked at him perched near the window sill. "You're coming to the werewolf house, too?"

"Of course. Someone's got to be the voice of reason." He fluffed his feathers, preening. "About Ami—remember, her father's keeping his distance. And, you know, for a god of communication? That guy has a tough time communicating. You've talked to him more than she has."

Ami's father was Hermes, the messenger of the gods. He was also believed to be a protector of thieves and was sometimes invoked by those who engaged in illegal or unethical practices. If that was still happening in this day and age, dude was probably pretty busy.

"Ever since Althea crafted that magic glass

cleaner for us to chat with folks in the underworld, Ami and Mom have talked a lot, so I think she's doing better. I mean, obviously, she's doing better."

"Yeah," Archie agreed, closing his eyes and nodding as his wings rustled against his body. "Things got dark for her. Even darker than the underworld—which turned out to be brighter and better decorated than I expected." He opened his eyes. "How are you and Jason doing with your bestie banter?"

"Our what now?" I asked, narrowing my eyes at the fluff of feathers before me.

"Your bestie banter? Soulmate sessions?" His wide, bright eyes stared, unblinking. "Love connections? What do you call them?"

I tilted my head and squinted, studying the owl before me. "Talks?"

"Talks," he echoed, nodding sagely. "That's what you're calling it. How patently uncreative, and yet so totally you." He seemed satisfied with my answer. "Well, whatever you call it, I hope it's going well."

Jason Bishop, my boyfriend, died in a...well, a Greek tragedy. Our relationship was far from perfect, as I valued my independence while he clung to his dependence. But now, none of that mattered.

He was dead, and I couldn't talk to ghosts unless I was sitting in front of a mirror.

"Jason and I still talk, but it's not the same as it used to be. He's trying to build a new life down there, and our conversations are dwindling week by week," I explained, pulling my hair back into a sleek ponytail with a black tie. "Besides, he's not thrilled that I'm spending time with Lothian, even though it's not like that."

"Not like what?"

"You know like what. The baby just adores him, so he's always around when I visit Emma." I shook my head quickly to ensure my hair was secure before shrugging my shoulders. I wasn't responsible for Hunter's attachment to Lothian, and Jason's jealousy was the least of my concerns.

Ami appeared in my doorway, her back straight and her expression confident. She was wearing a pale yellow dress that flowed around her ankles and a pair of strappy sandals. "Astra, are you ready?" she asked.

"Am I ready? I am." I tilted my head. "Why are you ready?"

"Althea and Ayla will stay here and handle the shop today. Aunt Gwennie thought it would be better if I came with you to Emma's." Seeing the expression on my face, Ami continued. "Ayla says she hasn't seen or heard from Mr. Fields, so with your psychometry and my cartomancy, we should better understand what's going on than they would. Or just you would."

"Right." I nodded. "Okay, then. Let's go solve a murder."

* * *

IF ARDEN HOUSE was a covenstead for a family of witches, the Wolf Creek house was a den for a pack of werewolves.

The Wolf Creek estate was home to five werewolves, Emma, and her son, Hunter. It stood tall and proud in the middle of a hill, surrounded by a sprawling green lawn and bushes. Acres of overgrown forest surrounded the property, with trees reaching for the sky and branches intertwining in a complex network. The house's walls were made of thick stone and surrounded by wild and untamed vegetation.

Honestly, it looked like a pack of werewolves lived there.

I didn't ask much about their pack of five men or why there were no female wolves. I didn't ask why none of the werewolves other than Eddie seemed to date or have relationships with women.

"This place is huge," Ami breathed as I parked my Jeep.

"They have a lot of land," I said. "I suspect it's so they can run as wolves without being seen by any of the neighbors. There aren't any wolves like them living naturally in the Florida wilds, and if someone came across them while walking their dog?" I slid off the seat and shut the door. "Well, there may be no wolves, but this is Florida. There are a lot of guns."

"Right."

Archie flew above us, flapping his wings loudly as he passed the trees and shrubs and glided over to settle on my shoulder. "Looks like the new Wolf Creek pack is doing well for themselves," he said. "They have land teeming with rabbits." Archie glared at Ami. "And rabbits that taste like they're supposed to. Not like they're booby-trapped to make a predator animal feel guilty about doing what a predator animal does."

"Savage," she told him.

"Predator," Archie corrected. "What will you do if a hawk shows up for you? Feed it kibble?"

Ami looked started. "What are you talking about?"

"Astra has me, so she didn't need a familiar. Ayla got Cerberus, the dimwitted dog, and Althea got Lily, the insulting crow. Your father is Hermes; his sacred animals are the tortoise, ram, and hawk." Archie tilted his head to the side. "He'd have to be an idiot to send you a ram. And he could have sent you a tortoise—maybe that's why it's so late getting here. It's a tortoise. They aren't exactly quick."

"Archie—"

"But my guess is that when your father gets around to sending you an animal, you'll find yourself with a hawk." Archie bobbed his head up and down, his eyes shining with amusement. "Likely a red-tailed hawk. And it will eat little furry animals." His beak was slightly opened as if he was holding back laughter.

Ami's face clouded with pain, and her eyebrows drew together in a frown. "My father hasn't called, stopped by, and he certainly hasn't sent me a familiar, so I doubt we need to worry about that any time soon." She averted her gaze from Archie, her face a mask of disappointment.

"You really just can't read the room, can you?" I scolded my awkward avian.

"We're not in a room."

Eddie opened the wooden front door just as my fist was about to make contact with it. "I saw you from the parapet. What are you two doing here? Did we have plans?"

I put aside my first question, which was why the werewolf estate had a parapet, and briefly told Eddie what I'd read as Ami handed him the paper. "I didn't know if Emma had seen the news anywhere yet."

Eddie gripped the paper tightly in both hands, his dark eyes fixed on the news. He moved quickly across the page as he absorbed the information, his brow furrowed and his lips pursed. "No. We don't get the newspaper here, and no one watches television much anymore." He raised his eyes. "The baby is more interesting."

"They don't talk, and they spew bodily fluids. That's interesting?" Archie asked.

Ami glared at Archie and took a deep breath before continuing. "I did an oracle card reading. I drew the Fool card, which means that Scarlett is innocent. There's no possibility she's guilty of what they claim." She hesitated before adding, "At least according to the reading. She didn't do this to her father and has no idea who did."

"Wouldn't Emma have heard about this from

Forkbridge PD?" I asked. I saw Eddie's face shift and flush a bit, his lips pressing together tightly as I asked the question.

He pulled out a phone I recognized as Emma's. "She's on maternity leave. I didn't want her bothered, so I hold on to it for her and let her run through it once a day."

"You let her?" My voice was sharp as I pointed out his unwarranted dominance over Emma. "What is she, twelve? What do you mean you 'let' her?"

"I manage it, so she isn't overwhelmed by the job and the baby," Eddie said evenly. "She needs to rest, and I help her with that."

"By controlling her?"

"It's just her phone, Astra. Come on." He held the phone up to show me. "I just don't want her to be bothered with all the stuff that goes on at the station." His eyes shifted away as he realized what he had said, and he quickly put the phone away. "You're right. I should have phrased it better. Sorry."

I bit back the urge to ask if that was what she wanted.

Because it wasn't just the phrasing.

He was clearly trying to protect Emma, and I couldn't fault him for that desire. But if the situation was reversed, Eddie would never have let Emma control his access to information outside the world.

But I kept my mouth shut.

It wasn't my job to tell Eddie how to live his life, and I wasn't sure it was my place to judge him, either.

He wasn't my boyfriend.

"Look, forget it. It's been a long day, and it's barely half past my coffee. We need to go tell her what happened and see what she can find out from Forkbridge PD."

Eddie stepped back cautiously, a slight hesitance in his expression and body language. "Come on in."

Ami and I followed his lead, and we entered the hallway together, the door closing softly behind us.

CHAPTER THREE

We entered the living room to find Emma surrounded by a stack of tiny onesies, pajamas, and blankets, a laundry basket by her feet on the floor. Despite the chaos, Emma's face lit up when she saw us, and she waved us over with a smile.

"Nice castle," I said, the corner of my lips twitching upward. "I read a steamy romance novel with this plot." I gestured toward the handsome and attentive men sitting at either side of Emma, their postures rigid as they waited for Emma to give the slightest need for them to act. I nodded in their direction, "Gentlemen."

Emma's boyfriend, Eddie Renzo, glanced at Wyatt Marlow and Norden Morris, two of his werewolf pack mates. "I'm pretty sure those books don't have an infant as the central character, and he most definitely is here."

As his tiny mouth opened to let out a tinkling giggle, the baby's eyes sparkled, and his lips formed an "O" of delight.

"If I didn't know better, I'd swear that kid knew what you said," Ami murmured.

"It's possible," Lothian announced as he entered the room and flopped down on the couch. "At eight weeks, wolf pups enter their juvenile period, and they start to follow the adults on hunting trips and can return to the den by themselves." He smiled. "Werewolves and half-werewolves have the advantage of developing faster than humans."

"Really?" I asked, the words dripping with sarcasm. "So, what went wrong with you?"

Archie snickered. "Good one."

"Thank you."

"What went wrong with me? Nothing." Lothian crossed his arms, and his lips curled into a sly smirk. "I am the perfect example of a werewolf. You recognize I'm the best of both worlds, a perfect amalgamation of human and wolf. Don't you?" He winked at me. "Even if you don't want to admit it."

"It's astounding the amount of confidence that you have," Archie said in a mocking voice. His feathered face showed a mixture of disgust and irritation. "I've spent centuries perfecting my haughty attitude, yet you have achieved it in the blink of an eye. Your self-importance is remarkable."

Lothian's lips twitched in amusement. "Why, thank you, divine one."

"It wasn't a compliment, you bonehead!"

The baby's laughter filled the room like a chorus of angelic bells. Eddie and Emma smiled at their son as Wyatt and Norden exchanged a look of amusement. Even Lothian, who had been arguing with Archie moments earlier, smiled at the baby's reaction.

Emma's eyes flickered between each of us. She placed Hunter in his bouncy seat, taking extra precautions to ensure he was secure. Afterward, she grabbed a towel from the basket and folded it into a neat square before returning her attention to us. "So what are you guys doing here? Did you miss the baby?"

Ami and I looked at each other.

"I can tell her if you want," she said.

"I got it." I held out the newspaper we'd brought with us. "It's about Mr. Fields, the guy you introduced us to yesterday at the farm? He died yesterday," I said. "After we left." I paused and waited for her to respond, but she didn't. "I'm sorry, Emma. I know how important he was to you."

"It can't be." Her face drained of color as she read the headline in the newspaper. She tried to muffle a sob, tears streaming down her face as she clutched the paper. The three men in the room, Eddie, Wyatt, and Norden, stood silently, their expressions grim and subdued. Lothian hung his head, unable to look at Emma as she grieved.

Hunter watched his mother, her eyes welling with tears, and soon his eyes began to brim with salty droplets. A slow, whimpering cry escaped his lips.

Eddie bent his knees and scooped his son up in one swift motion. "I got you, buddy," he said, cradling the tiny baby in his muscled arm. "Mommy's okay."

"Murdered? It can't be!" Emma's eyes widened as she scanned the story. Her mouth dropped open as she read the news, her forehead creasing in confusion. She stared at the paper for a few more moments before looking up. "This can't be right. They arrested Scarlett?"

"They did."

"What the hell are they thinking?"

"That she did it," Ami answered. "But she didn't do it, Emma. That's why we're here. I did a reading, and I'm sure that Scarlett didn't kill her father."

"Well, of course, she didn't do it!"

Eddie held Hunter close, swaying and cooing to soothe him. The infant's tears had dried up, replaced by a fit of fierce anger. His cherubic face scrunched up as he voiced his protests with a chorus of unintelligible gibberish.

Emma's eyes flashed with anger. She pulled her phone out of her pocket, and I watched as she jabbed at the screen with her finger. Finally, she lifted the gadget to her ear, her lips pressed together in a tight line.

"Chief, what the hell is going on? How could you arrest Scarlett Fields?" she exclaimed, her voice ringing with frustration.

We watched Emma in tense silence as she listened to Chief Harmon, her brows furrowed and lips pursed in concentration. Her eyes flicked back and forth, and her cheeks flushed pink as her emotions shifted and changed.

"This is unacceptable!" she yelled into the receiver. "The driveway is in Forkbridge! I don't care if half the farm is in the unincorporated part of the county. They had no right to take over jurisdiction!" A pause. "The address is in Forkbridge, and our department should handle the case, not theirs!"

The baby fussed in his father's arms, his tiny fists beating against Eddie's chest. No matter how much his father rocked him back and forth, Hunter would not be consoled and gurgled even more angry gibberish.

Meanwhile, Emma remained silent, her expression hardening with every word from Chief Harmon. She didn't respond except for the occasional grunt or huff of disbelief, her lips pressed together in a thin line. After a few moments of tense silence, she spoke softly into the receiver and then hung up.

"Well?" I asked.

Emma looked around at us, her expression a mixture of concern and resignation, before finally speaking up.

"The Strawberry Fields Farm is only partially in Forkbridge," she explained. "Mr. Fields' body was found in the part of the farm that falls outside of Forkbridge's town limits and instead falls under the jurisdiction of the unincorporated county. Or so they claimed, even though I've never heard of such ridiculous bull. One of the county deputies has taken over the case."

* * *

VOLUSIA COUNTY HAD IGNORED our area for the most part—Daytona Beach presented much easier problems to deal with, such as drunk kids and beach-related mishaps.

The oddities of our small towns and creepy swamps, with their strange psychic people, haunting ghosts, and occasional bizarre mythological creatures, were simply not their problem.

As weird as it sounds, it was almost a blessing in disguise.

"Deputy Mason Abernathy is the newest addition to the sheriff's office," Emma explained. "According to Chief Harmon, Abernathy is a metaphysician, and the county hired him specifically to oversee the strange happenings in our 'paranormally tainted' tiny towns."

"A metaphysician? What the heck is that?" I exclaimed in disbelief.

Lothian's eyes narrowed in confusion. "Yeah, what does that even mean?"

Ami quickly swiped her thumb across her

phone, her face illuminated by the blue light of its screen. "Webster's says a metaphysician is a student of or specialist in metaphysics," she explained. Then, after a brief pause, she looked up at us. "So basically, everyone we know is a metaphysician?"

Norden looked deeply concerned. "Why does this Abernathy guy have jurisdiction over a murder in Forkbridge?" he asked. "The farm is technically in Forkbridge, isn't it?"

"Technically, yes, but no," Emma said. "The county can intervene if the town's police force isn't equipped to handle a case. The chief said Deputy Abernathy is the one who decided to take over Mr. Fields' murder investigation." She frowned. "He's also arguing that it happened on the county's side of the property, but I think he's only doing that to cover his snatching of the case."

Eddie's forehead furrowed into a deep frown. "So what do we do now?" he asked, his voice laced with concern.

"Go to the sheriff's office and talk to this Deputy Abernathy?" I suggested.

Emma nodded in agreement. "Yes, I think that's our best course of action. I can offer my help as a detective in Forkbridge—"

Before she could finish her sentence, Eddie cut her off.

"You're on maternity leave," he reminded her firmly. "There's no way you should be involved in this. Let us handle it. I've been in law enforcement just as long as you have, and I can handle it just fine while you stay home with Hunter."

I could have sworn I heard baby Hunter's voice pipe up with a faint "uh oh."

Emma's eyes narrowed, and her lips pursed as she whirled around to face Eddie. Her fists were clenched at her sides, and she looked ready to give him a piece of her mind.

Eddie blinked in surprise, taken aback by Emma's sudden change in demeanor. "Look, Emma—" he began to say, but she cut him off with a wave.

Emma's face was a mixture of determination and indignation as she spoke, her voice full of passion. "You know nothing about Strawberry Fields Farm," she told Eddie. "You haven't been going there multiple times a year for over thirty years. You didn't know Mr. Fields. You don't know Scarlett. You don't know anything about it or the people who work there. You've never worked in this county, and you're not currently an employee of this town's law enforcement. You have no badge. So explain why it makes sense for you to deal with this, not me?"

Eddie's voice caught in his throat as he began to speak, his eyes widening at realizing his misstep. "Emma, I meant—"

"No," Emma interrupted. "You may think you know what's best here, even though this isn't your town and these aren't your people. But you don't know a thing," she spat out, her hands on her hips. Her voice was filled with biting sarcasm that cut through the air like a knife.

Hunter's small and unassuming fist made contact with Eddie's nose with surprising force. The big detective winced in pain, clearly taken aback by the infant's sudden attack.

"I feel like we should have called first," Archie said from my shoulder, his voice tinged with amusement. "This must be family fight day."

"Be quiet, rudeness," I whispered.

Eddie rubbed his nose and glanced down at his son, who stared at him with wide, innocent eyes. "Hunter's got your back, I see," he chuckled, shaking his head in disbelief. "That was quite a wallop, there, son."

Emma did not chuckle.

She did not look amused.

I stared at Eddie Renzo in disbelief, shocked that he couldn't summon up the two words he needed to say to head off this lover's spat. "Just say you're sorry, Eddie," I thought, frustrated by his stubbornness. "It's not only about you getting it. It's about you realizing you were wrong and disrespectful and making her feel you were deciding for her. Tell her you're sorry, dude. Come on."

I could see that Eddie felt it too. His face showed a mix of embarrassment, guilt, and regret. He looked apologetic and determined not to let Emma down again, but he still couldn't find the words to express his feelings.

In the end, he just didn't say it. And I couldn't help but feel a twinge of disappointment as I watched their tension continue to simmer.

"Nothing else to say?" she prompted, doing everything but drawing the poor guy a roadmap.

Eddie shook his head, a somber expression on his face. "I'm sorry," he said quietly. "I just figured you wanted to stay with Hunter. If you didn't, you would have returned to work by now. I just thought you chose Hunter over work, but I shouldn't have assumed—"

I winced, feeling a pang of sympathy for Eddie. He was trying to make amends, but his words still fell short of a genuine apology. Emma's expression remained stony, and I could tell she wasn't convinced he knew what he'd done.

Emma gave him a stern glare. "You should have stopped with the apology," she told him, crossing her arms over her chest. "Just drop it, okay? I'm going, and this conversation is over. You'll watch the baby."

Eddie nodded. "Okay. And yeah, I should have."

The tension in the room dissipated a bit, and I let out a long breath.

"So…" Emma said, looking around the group. "Deputy Abernathy?"

* * *

I GLANCED in my rearview mirror and saw Lothian and Wyatt riding their motorcycles close behind us. The chrome of their handlebars gleamed in the afternoon sun. "Doesn't he know we can see him trailing us?" I asked Emma, shifting my gaze from the werewolves to her in the backseat.

Emma shook her head from the backseat and said, "It's pretty obvious they're following us."

Emma's stern look remained, her brows furrowed and her lips pressed together. "By the way, don't think I didn't notice you said 'him' and not 'them' when talking about our werewolf pack security detail. I know this isn't the time to bring it up, but if I do, maybe you won't ask me what's happening with Eddie and me."

I felt a sudden wave of embarrassment as she called me out on my slip-up. "Oh," I said, nodding in understanding. "I can see that. So, what's going on with you and Eddie?"

Ami chuckled.

"We've been having some problems lately, and I'm not sure how to fix them." Emma sighed and rolled her eyes. "He's just been acting like an overprotective caveman lately. Like, it's the twenty-first century, you know? I don't need someone to coddle me and always tell me what to do. I can make my own decisions. I swear, it's like my brother all over again. It's ridiculous, too—did you know that in wolf packs, both males and females protect the pack? So there's no excuse for this. None."

Ami turned from the passenger seat, her voice hinting caution. "Well, that's true, but there are exceptions. Male wolves may take on a protective role toward female wolves. Especially during the breeding season when the females are pregnant or caring for their young."

"Okay, Althea," I joked.

"I hate when you do that. I read, too."

"You're right," I admitted. "I'm sorry."

"Oh, who cares what you people read about wolves? They're not wolves," Emma snapped, her lips forming a thin line as she stared out the window into the darkening sky.

Ami blinked. "Well, no, but you just said...."

My sister trailed off as I brought my finger to my lips and tapped them in a universal sign for silence.

Ami was about to answer Emma's ill-conceived emotional rant with a hefty dose of logic, and I doubted the annoyed new mother was in the mood for any of that.

"Right. Sorry," Ami said, apologizing to Emma.

My best bud was irritated by Eddie's behavior, but there was also sadness in her voice as she spoke about it.

I glanced at her in the mirror and cleared my throat. "Maybe, if you two sit down and talk about this together, you can work toward finding some common ground."

My friend rolled her eyes at me, her lips twitching in a smirk. "Astra?"

"Yep?"

"Shut up."

I sighed. "Yes, ma'am."

Emma shifted in the back seat, her frustration palpable. "Ugh, seriously?" she exclaimed, her voice tinged with exasperation. "They won't leave us alone. Stupid Neanderthal motorcycle werewolves. It feels like we're starring in our own version of The Handmaid's Tale. Can't leave the house without chaperones."

Ami turned to stare at Emma, her expression incredulous. "You must be kidding," she said, her voice rising with indignation. "You're comparing someone caring about you so much that they're sending their people out to guard you against harm to women being used as baby machines against their will in a dystopia? Seriously?"

I could hear the fiery passion in my sister's voice as she challenged Emma's comparison. When I glanced at her, I could see her eyes blazing with pain and defiance.

I glanced at Emma next and found her looking taken aback by Ami's reaction, her eyes widening in surprise. "I didn't mean it like that," she said.

"My mom raised us in a house that served as a temple to a goddess hardly remembered. My mother trained us to be priestesses for a goddess that twenty or so people came to worship occasionally. And because I had to serve in that capacity, I never had the chance or choice to attend school, meet my father, or have a boyfriend. I never experienced what it's like to have someone love me so much that they were tripping all over themselves to protect me." Ami's gaze was steady. "Believe me when I say I'd swap places and problems with you in a heartbeat, Emma Sullivan."

We rode silently for a few moments, the tension in the car palpable.

Finally, Emma spoke up, her voice contrite. "I'm sorry, Ami," she said. "I didn't mean to trivialize your experiences by cracking jokes about mine."

Ami looked at Emma for a moment before nodding. "It's all right. I get why you said what you did. Everyone has their stories, and we all look at the world through our own lenses, which can make it hard to see it from anyone else's perspective."

Emma nodded, her expression softening. "Thanks," she said.

Pulling into the sheriff's office parking lot, I checked the rearview mirror one last time. The werewolves were still following us, and I knew they would stay even after we arrived at our destination—which was driving Emma crazy.

I couldn't help but agree with my sister Ami, though.

Having an escort of protective werewolves was a pretty nice problem to have.

CHAPTER FOUR

$\mathcal{W}$e stepped out of the car and made our way into the sheriff's office. The werewolves had parked several spots away, their eyes fixed on us as we made our way to the entrance. I could still feel Lothian's eyes on my back as we stepped inside.

The sheriff's office looked like a small, unassuming building from the outside, but inside, it was bustling with activity. People milled about, talking in hushed voices while staring at wooden desks piled high with paperwork. Filing cabinets and shelves of books lined every wall of the large square room. The windows were too small, so only a little light came through to alleviate the dim drabness.

"Cheerful place," I said.

"I'd go crazy working here," Emma muttered. "One should never consider gun metal gray as a decorative choice, in any circumstances."

Emma stepped forward, and we advanced toward the front desk.

The young deputy behind the counter—Deputy Harris, according to his name badge—seemed to jolt when he caught sight of us, his eyes scanning with a mixture of curiosity and suspicion. "Can I help you?" he asked, his tone wary.

Always nice to feel welcome.

"We're here to see Deputy Abernathy," Emma said, her voice firm. "I heard he was working the Fields case, and I wanted to offer my help." She pulled out her badge and flashed it. "I'm Detective Emma Sullivan, and I've known the Fields family for thirty years now."

"And you think the fact that you're buddies with the murderer makes you ideal for offering your wisdom on our case, Detective?" As Deputy Harris said the word 'detective,' his voice filled with disdain and dripped with contempt. "And why bring an entourage with you? Were you ladies swinging by on your way to a spa day?" He chuckled. "Or a day at the beach?"

My hands were practically twitching with the urge to give this fool a good slap.

Emma spun around and gave me a look of stunned disbelief. She then shifted her gaze back to the sassy sheriff's deputy. "Excuse me?" she hissed like a teapot on a stove.

"Oh, calm down." The deputy's laugh was overemphasized and filled with arrogance as if he were mocking Emma even further. "Don't get your panties in a wad. Make yourselves comfortable. I'll let him know you're here."

We found a seat in the corner and waited.

"Wow. What was that guy's problem?" Ami asked.

"Overconfidence," I said.

"Arrogance," Emma added.

"But why?"

"Look around this office, Ami. Take in all of it. Who's here, how it's decorated, what's happening," Emma told her. "What do you see? Or, more importantly, what don't you see in this office?"

My eyes darted around the room until I struck on the something peculiar Emma was trying to point out; we were the only women in the entire office. Everyone else was male, either young or middle-aged.

"There are no women," Ami said.

"Exactly. It's a good old boys club," Emma said. "I can guess who these guys are. Men who have been here for years and years, men not interested in making room for new blood or different ideas. I'm sure they don't like feeling challenged by women. Or having to answer to them. Or having them suggest they might be able to help them."

A door across the room creaked open, and in strode a tall man, face carved from granite and eyes as hard as gems. His uniform was so crisp that it looked as if it could cut glass, and his hat gleamed in the few rays of light that managed to get into this place. His cowboy boots thumped on the ground with each step.

Deputy Abernathy had arrived.

And boy, did we know it.

The room's energy shifted the second he stepped into it, like a lightning bolt had struck. All conversations screeched to a halt as everyone tracked his movements, eyes glued to his every step. A faint smirk curved his lips as he paraded around, his steely eyes inspecting us with an oddly menacing curiosity.

It was creepy.

He was creepy.

Deputy Harris stood tall at his post, hands clasped behind his back, chin held high. He nodded slyly toward Deputy Abernathy with a mischievous glint in his eye. "The ladies I told you about, boss."

He stood before us like a monolith, peering down his nose at us with a scowl on his face as though daring us to make the slightest misstep.

"I'm Deputy Abernathy," he said, his voice gruff. "What can I do for you?"

Emma stood up and reached her hand out to shake his, her voice strong and sure. "We came to offer our assistance on the Fields case. I'm Detective Emma Sullivan, and I've known the family for over thirty years. I normally work over in the Forkbridge PD, but I've been on maternity leave recently. I imagine that's why you took over the case from our department."

"I see," Deputy Abernathy said, his face unreadable as he studied Emma with a cool, measured gaze. "You imagine that, do you?"

Emma stood, hand extended.

Abernathy did not take it.

I stole a quick glance at Detective Abernathy's hand, my eyes drawn to a subtle yet telling detail. There, on his ring finger, was a faint indentation, the ghostly echo of a wedding band that had once encircled his finger. Recently divorced?

He examined Emma for a long moment, his eyes searching her face. It was as if he was trying to assess her, to determine whether she was a friend or foe. Then he turned his gaze to me and finally to Ami. "Come with me," he said finally, stepping aside and pointing toward the door he'd arrived through. "Let's discuss this in my office."

He turned and headed for the door without another word.

"Astra," Ami whispered.

I turned toward her.

She held up the Emperor card. "He was giving me this creepy feeling, so I pulled a card. He's convinced he's doing the right thing, but he's using his power to make other people do what he wants."

Emma, overhearing Ami, turned back. "I hate to tell you this, but that's not super uncommon. Cops have to be pretty confident and feel like they're ethical in what they do. But that swagger can turn into a monster pretty fast if they're not watching themselves. Some people do use the job as an excuse to get their power fix, I'm sorry to say."

"Yeah, maybe," Ami said.

She didn't seem convinced.

* * *

WE FOLLOWED Deputy Abernathy into his office.

Deputy Abernathy cleared his throat as we entered, knocking on the large desk that dominated his space as if for good luck. There were few personal accents in the office. Just several filing cabinets lined up against the bland-colored walls—walls that were bare except for several certificates of recognition and a few diplomas.

I squinted, but they were far enough away that I couldn't read them.

Deputy Abernathy sat down in the chair behind the desk and motioned for us to take a seat despite the office only having two more in front of his desk. Ami leaned against the door frame with her arms crossed, a silent indication Emma and I would take the lead in this conversation.

We sat down.

After studying us for a moment, as if sizing us up, he spoke. "So, you want to help with the Fields case?" Abernathy leaned back in his chair, steepling his fingers together. "You do understand in a case of this magnitude, we have to be very careful about who we bring on board. I don't want to risk any potential conflicts of interest or any potential for bias."

I saw a subtle change in Abernathy's features —his eyes darkened, his lip curled up ever so slightly, and his mouth pinched shut as if he were holding back a sinister smirk. He leaned to one side, his steepled hands drifting closer to his sidearm. Those small movements seemed to suggest a deeper plotting, and the cold glint in his eyes sent a chill down my spine.

This man did not like us.

Not at all.

"Yes, we do," Emma said. "But we're here to offer our help and expertise, not to make any decisions on the case. I understand the importance of due process, I know how to follow procedures, and, as I mentioned, I am a detective. We're just here to help."

"Your brother is Rex Sullivan."

I felt my shoulders tense as the conversation took a sudden turn, and my alertness heightened as if I had almost stepped on a rattlesnake.

"Rex?" Emma asked, confused.

His gaze shifted to me, then back to Emma. "Isn't that right? The man that owns that club by the highway? That's your brother, isn't it?" Deputy Abernathy drawled out the word "man" in a slow, deliberate manner, his contempt for Rex evident in the way he rolled the syllables of the word across his tongue. "What's that place called—Sanguine?" His hands remained steepled together as if in silent judgment, and his posture remained unchanged.

Alarm bells were beginning to ring in my head.

Emma took a deep breath before answering. "Yes, Rex is my brother, and Sanguine's his club, but I'm not sure what that has to do with our offer to help you with background information on the case."

Deputy Abernathy leaned back in his chair, his eyes narrowed. "You don't, do you?" He narrowed his eyes, the left corner of his mouth twitching, as he swept his gaze back and forth between Emma and me. I could feel his silent condemnation in the air like a thick fog. "What if I told you there was an occult symbol written in the dirt next to Mr. Fields' dead body? Would that jar your pretty little head in making a possible connection between your brother's club and the murder scene?"

"What kind of symbol?" Ami blurted out.

I wanted to turn around and tell Ami to stay quiet, but I didn't want to give the crazy guy more kindling for his fire of paranoia and delusions.

"What kind of symbol?" Abernathy's eyes drifted between Emma and me and Ami in a rhythmic sweep, narrowing and widening with the speed of a camera shutter. "I told you, didn't I? An occult symbol." He leaned forward and tapped his index finger on the desk as if emphasizing his point. "Most people wouldn't bother to ask for more specifics than that. You know who would?"

The air was crackling with anticipation, like the time delay on a firework, making everyone eagerly await the huge explosion. I suspected this explosion, though, had the potential to cause more trouble than joy.

Abernathy leaned forward, his voice low and menacing. "Witches. Witches would ask." The unease snapped like a rubber band. "Witches would want to know."

I carefully reached down to the chair, my fingers moving slowly until I could feel the cool, smooth texture of the seat. I closed my eyes and, with a deep breath, allowed my hand to curl around it. Instantly, an image filled my mind—

Deputy Abernathy and Deputy Harris flanked by a mysterious man I couldn't recognize. A heated conversation was taking place between them, and it seemed to be escalating.

In the fog of the vision, Abernathy's face was as red as an overripe tomato, and his eyes glimmered with indignation. He slammed his fist down onto his desk and declared, "No more of these low-down devils in this county! We are gonna show 'em who's boss!" He threw his head back, sticking his chin out proudly as a fine spray of saliva flew from his mouth.

A booming voice jolted me back to reality.

"Open your eyes and show me your hands this instant, sorceress!"

I rolled my eyes (while my lids were still closed because it's important not to provoke a crazy person) and then opened them, locking stares with Deputy Abernathy.

Abernathy looked across at me with an expression of hatred and contempt, his eyes alight with fury. "You'll do as I say!" He pointed his finger at me. "And you'll do it now!"

I really wanted to yawn in his face.

But I didn't.

"You're literally looking into my eyes." I released my grip on the chair, my fingers curling into fists. I held them up in front of me, never looking away from the jerk's calculating eyes. I wanted him to know I wouldn't back down.

"I know who and what you are," Deputy Abernathy said, his face flushed and his lips curled in an angry snarl. "I've been hired to deal with you people and your dangerous agenda. And I'll do it, too. Luck is on my side—I haven't even been here two weeks, and one of you fell into my lap."

One of us?

The deputy's stare was intense, and his eyes blazed with a fit of righteous anger that almost seemed to emit light, as if he was burning from the inside. "Did you think I would let some harlot that lives with a pack of werewolves join my investigation? And bring two witches from the Central Florida version of the Mayfair witches along with her to boot? What do you take me for?"

Someone that's never had a real relationship with a woman, I thought.

Emma's face was a mask of calm, her expression guarded and unreadable. "Deputy Abernathy, I assure you—"

"You can assure me of nothing. How do I know you didn't kill Fields to defend your little witch friend Scarlett? Scarlett. Named after the very letter we tattoo onto evil women!" His fists clenched and unclenched, his knuckles turning white with the effort. "I know what your brother is, too, little girl. What they all are at that club. You have the nerve to show your face here?"

I could feel my face flush red, my fury rising within me like a storm.

If this guy ever saw or read or watched The Scarlet Letter, I would sing karaoke in public without any alcohol. And if he did see it or read it, he missed the point.

It wasn't puritan fanfic.

"Deputy Abernathy, we completely respect your authority and your investigation," Emma said, her voice even and calm in an attempt to bring the sexist simian down from his bigot branch. "But we won't be intimidated. We've come here today to offer our assistance, not to be judged. But if you don't want our help, then we'll leave. There's no need for accusations or escalations."

He had other ideas.

"Submit yourselves!" Deputy Abernathy boomed. "Resist the devil, and he will flee from you! Change from your ways, and this will no longer be a blighted place full of unspeakable creatures!"

Deputy Abernathy scrunched up his face as if to start blabbering again, but I wasn't having it. I rose up and declared, "That's enough. We're done. Thanks for the chit-chat."

Without another word, we left.

* * *

THE SECOND OUR feet hit the pavement outside of the stuffy building, Ami took a deep breath and rolled her eyes, her slight shoulders dropping as the tension left her frame. "Way too much intensity in there," she muttered as if she was trying to blow out the last bit of knotted stress that still lingered. "At least now I have a better appreciation of what the crusades felt like."

"You do not," I told her. "We got to walk out. We were not put in a cage and tossed into the swamp."

"What a jerk," Emma muttered, shaking her head in disbelief.

"A jerk that knows this area has witches, vampires, and werewolves," I pointed out as we walked across the parking lot toward Lothian and Wyatt. None of us discussed bypassing my Jeep and heading straight for the werewolves we hadn't wanted on this journey, anyway, but we all did it. "A blighted place full of unspeakable creatures. That's actually not a bad nickname for Central Florida."

Ami glared at me. "Knock it off. That was rude."

"What I don't understand is how he knew Eddie and the guys were werewolves. I mean, they just moved here," Emma said as we walked up to the two motorcycles. "Rex I can kind of understand. He's pale with ruby-red lips and only comes out at night. I mean, it doesn't take a metaphysician or whatever that guy calls himself to put two and two together."

"Don't forget he named his club Sanguine," Ami added.

Lothian scrunched up his nose. "That just means optimistic."

"It also means blood red."

"Oof. Okay, that was a little more in-your-face than he needed to be."

"I know, right?"

Archie circled overhead and then descended, talons outstretched, to land on my shoulder with a dramatic flourish. "Did you see anything?" He cocked his head to one side. "You know, with the magic you were born with that you keep stuffed in your pocket?"

I nodded. "I did, in fact. I read the chair."

"Will wonders never cease?"

I spilled the tea about my vision to the squad, and Ami brought up her strange vibe and her scary pull of the Emperor card. Emma finished by relating the crux of the uncomfortable meeting. "So, yeah, he's going to be a problem."

"I don't understand. He's literally on a witch hunt?" Wyatt asked, his expression grim. "This isn't the Dark Ages. Not many humans are stupid enough to do this kind of thing. No one has persecuted anyone for being a witch in hundreds of years. Well, not by the humans, anyway. Your old associates were..." His voice trailed off, and he glanced at me with a meaningful look.

"Deposed, so let's drop it."

Wyatt nodded. "Consider it dropped."

"Man, you fold to her so easy," Lothian told Wyatt.

Wyatt pointed. "You know she has god lightning in her fingertips, right?"

"She'd never zap me."

Lothian seemed far too confident of that, so I jolted him gently with a spark of star energy and kept talking. "You heard the guy. In his head, he's been appointed as the county's hero and aims to rid the community of any 'undesirables.'" Taking my gaze away from Lothian, I looked at Emma. "Though I don't understand what his reasoning was for the rant and rave or arrest. Scarlett isn't a witch, so some of what he said doesn't make sense."

"She's not a witch like you, no," Emma said, her brows knitting as she squinted at the dreary structure, "but she did get into nature religions and pagan stuff and Wicca when she was in college. Maybe that's what he meant."

"Right, remember?" Ami said. "Ayla knew her from our shop."

Wyatt frowned. "It's not the same, though."

"Would he know the difference?" Archie asked.

"That's not the question. Even if he knew, would he care?" I asked. "After spending a decidedly unpleasant few minutes with Deputy Witchfinder in there, I'd guess probably not." I looked at Emma. "I think we need to see this occult symbol-ed crime scene for ourselves. Before talking to Scarlett."

She paused, thought, and then nodded. "Agreed."

As the wolves revved up the engines of their

motorcycles and we climbed into my Jeep, I couldn't shake the feeling that Deputy Abernathy's arrival was too conveniently timed.

The guy's been on the job less than two weeks, and he "uncovered" an occult murder committed by a witch at a wholesome family tourist spot?

I mean, come on.

Central Florida really was teaming with paranormals around every corner and under every rock, and we'd managed to head most murders off.

But him?

Less than two weeks, and he got who he was gunning for?

No way.

Too convenient.

With a deep breath, I turned the ignition, and we drove off toward the farm, unsure of what awaited us at our destination.

CHAPTER FIVE

We drove in silence toward the Strawberry Fields Farm, the weight of our thoughts heavy in the car. As we pulled up to the farm, it was clear that things had changed since the last time we visited.

The once bustling family farm was now eerily quiet.

The sun hung in the crisp blue sky, its golden rays filtering through the clouds as the three of us stepped out of the Jeep and stretched our limbs. "This place looks so peaceful," Emma said, taking a deep breath.

The hustle and bustle of families running to pick berries or take a hayride had disappeared into memory as the farm closed to the public.

Only a few county police officers and workers milling around, watching, could be seen near the strawberry field.

"Looks can be deceiving," I warned, already on alert. I looked up and spotted Archie circling overhead, his wings outstretched as he rode the thermals. His eyes scanned the field below, looking for any signs of danger or trouble.

Lothian strolled up and remarked, "You know what? I prefer this place when it's not overrun with people."

"I'm sure they prefer to be somewhere you're not, too," I told him.

Lothian tilted his head and pursed his lips, blinking as he asked, "Why do you gotta be so mean to me?" His eyes glinted in the dim light, a mocking expression of woundedness at odds with the smirk on his face.

I didn't answer.

A moment later, Wyatt joined us, scanning the field for potential threats. "Looks like things are quiet for the moment," he said, his voice hushed. "We're being watched, though." Wyatt pointed toward the barn.

Brock Taylor stood motionless in the barn doorway, his silhouette framed by dim lights within the building. His hands were in his pockets, and he surveyed us with heavy eyes, his face an unreadable mask.

"That's Brock Taylor, Mr. Fields' right-hand man," Emma told us. "He's been working here for the last decade or so. As Mr. Fields aged, Taylor took on more responsibility for running the farm."

"That's the guy Scarlett said her dad was thinking about leaving the farm to instead of her, right?" I asked.

Emma nodded.

We watched Brock, and I could feel Ami tense up beside me for no particular reason I could discern. Then again, we were close to a murder scene. I couldn't recall Ami being with me in a situation like that before.

I looked up as Archie screeched.

The tranquil stillness was interrupted by the thunderous rumble of a diesel engine. In a matter of moments, a worn-out red truck emerged on the horizon, billowing a haze of dust as it approached.

"That's Henry Johnson," Emma told us.

"Who's Henry Johnson?"

"He manages Johnson Farms and provides berries to many local grocery stores," she said as she watched him exit his truck. It bore the unmistakable label of "Johnson Farms" in bold white letters on the side. "Unlike this place, it's not a tourist destination. Just a working farm."

Henry Johnson, a tall and handsome man in his midthirties, had an outdoorsy look to him in his jeans, plaid shirt, and work boots. His tanned skin and muscular frame suggested a life of hard physical work, but he didn't seem any worse for it. His dark hair was cut neatly short, and his piercing stare could probably get him a few dances at Rex's club without a problem.

He moved toward us, his long strides fueled by a surge of adrenaline. His broad chest led the way, and his heavy boots pounded the ground with each step. We were so engrossed in watching him come toward us that we failed to notice Brock Taylor slip into our circle from the other side.

"Let me make it clear, this here is a real working farm."

Startled by his sudden appearance, our eyes moved toward him in unison.

"Whatever else we do, we grow and harvest food." Brock looked sideways at Emma. "Do not disrespect the hardworking men that work here by belittling their efforts like this is some kind of amusement park."

"Hardworking men?" I caught Brock's gendered compliment and decided not to let it pass. "Do the women that work here not work as hard? Or are there no women working here now that Scarlett Fields is in jail?"

Henry Johnson joined the group, and without any formal introduction, he spoke up. "Scarlett Fields, and every woman present, work as hard if not harder than any man here, no matter how much Taylor may deny it." He paused, his finger pointing at Brock, the tallest of the men in our odd little circle. "She was the brains behind this operation, keeping everything running. She made sure there was food for the local market as well as berries to pick for the kids."

Brock glared at Henry. "You're trespassing."

"You know damn well I'm not. And you can't deny anything I said."

"I'm the backbone of this operation." Brock frowned. "The girl worked a jam stand."

"See what I mean?" Henry's piercing gaze moved from one of us to the next, punctuating his words. "The 'girl' is the same age as you and me, and she grew up on this farm. You, Mr. Mainsplain, are a misogynist who did nothing but give Scarlett grief the moment you set yourself up as some kind of heir apparent. Like you have some kind of authority over her just because you showed up here."

Brock glared at him. "What are you doing here, Johnson?"

"Checking on my berry fields," he said with a shrug. "Same as you, I guess."

The atmosphere in the gravel parking lot was tense as the two men stood on either side of the impromptu gathering. Their eyes locked in a silent battle; all of us surrounding them could sense the tension. The spoken and unspoken animosity was palpable.

Brock's teeth ground together, his fists clenched tightly as he glared at Henry Johnson. After a moment of tense silence, he muttered something that sounded like, "I'm done here," before turning and stomping off. The barn door slammed shut with a final echo of his anger, leaving us in a heavy silence.

Emma watched Brock storm off, throwing his arms up in the air, and she shook her head. "Well," she muttered under her breath, "that went about as well as a penguin on roller skates."

* * *

"I CAN'T STAND THAT GUY," Henry Johnson muttered.

"You don't say?" I raised my eyebrows. "The hostility isn't exactly subtle, Mr. Johnson."

"That's because the guy is a jerk, and he deserves it," Henry said, his eyes still on the barn. "He's been like that since he started working here. He's always been jealous of Scarlett, and it's gotten worse the older her dad got. He thinks he should be the one running this place because he's a man. That kind of misogynistic bull infuriates me."

"Mr. Johnson, why do you—"

"Call me Henry," he said, his eyes still focused on the spot where Brock had disappeared.

Emma began introducing us to Henry Johnson like they were old friends. "This is Astra, and that's Ami. I'm Emma." She continued on and smiled briefly as she finished her sentence.

Henry studied Emma and then shifted his gaze to me. "You both used to work for the Forkbridge Police Department, didn't you?" He stroked his chin. "Astra, you're that psychic that can find lost objects or something, right? And you partnered with Emma when she used to work there?"

"I still do work there," Emma said. She held up her badge. "I'm on maternity leave."

"I don't work for the department anymore," I said shortly. "I got fired."

"Congratulations on your new baby!" Henry smiled at Emma. Glancing at me, he frowned and said, "Sorry about the job."

I shrugged. "It beats getting shot in aisle five of Punktex, I guess. Which was my ex-boyfriend's mother's other option to get even with me."

Henry nodded with recognition. "Right. That was you, wasn't it?"

I nodded.

Yep, that was me.

"Now that we've all been introduced, care to tell us what brings you here?" Emma inquired, her tone shifting from friendly to Detective Emma (who was only a step away from extracting a confession for the candy you stole in first grade.)

"I have a contract with Strawberry Fields Farm for berries." He sighed and wiped his forehead with the back of his hand. "I have the right to inspect the facilities and fields whenever I want by that contract, so here I am." He let out a long breath and lowered his voice. "I saw Scarlett this morning, and Brock Taylor told her attorney that he wouldn't allow her to look around here."

I looked at Emma. "Can he do that?"

"Probably not, but he's legally in possession of the farm right now since Scarlett's in jail and Mr. Fields is dead. Until that will is read, we won't know who owns the farm—"

"Which will?" Henry asked.

We all turned to him.

"Scarlett has a will saying she's the heir. Now, her father was threatening to change it because she was single, but he hadn't changed it yet. If he was going to." He shook his head and turned away from the barn, his expression a mix of disappointment and anger. "I knew Barry since I was a teenager. Despite his old-fashioned ways, Mr. Fields put a lot of faith in Scarlett, and he loved her. A lot. And when it came down to it, there was no way Barry would cut out his own daughter." He frowned. "And yet—"

"There's a will that says Brock Taylor inherits everything," Emma said. "Two wills. Two heirs."

"Yes." Henry raised an eyebrow. "How did you know that?"

"I didn't. I had a feeling," she replied, her lips curving down. "Since he has possession, the attorney probably needs to go to court to get access to the farm." Emma looked around. "That can take a while."

They say murder is a crime of passion, but from my experience, it's often driven by something far more mundane. Money and inheritance are two of the most common motives for taking someone's life. It's a sad—but undeniable—truth.

Two wills.

Two suspects.

One suspect is in jail, and one is in control of the crime scene.

"Is that why Brock didn't throw us off the property?" I asked. "Because we were with you?"

"Probably." Henry shrugged. "Maybe he thought I called you guys to meet me here. Brock Taylor may have control of this farm right now, but he has to let me onto the property. Me and anyone I bring with me. If he doesn't, he's got to pay a pretty hefty fine. I insisted on that in the contract."

"Is that normal?"

"For me? Absolutely," he said, flashing a troubled smile. "I'm a bit of a stickler when it comes to details in contracts. I don't want to be selling fruit harvested by exploited labor. The only way I can ensure that doesn't happen is by reserving the right to access the farm whenever I need to."

"Seems like you've got things under control."

Henry shrugged. "It pays off in the end." He glanced up at the sky, squinting at the position of the sun. "Look, I think we're both here for the same thing—to find what they don't want Scarlett's attorney to see. You're more than welcome to come with me, but if you're going to, we should move. It's getting late, and I want to check out the 'condition of the fields'"—Henry made air quotes with his hands—"before the sun sets."

With that, he turned and started walking toward the strawberries.

"Can we check out the barn, too?" Emma asked.

Henry stopped and looked at her. "You think we'll find something?"

"I don't know," she admitted. "But it's worth a shot. We're here."

I nodded in agreement. "If there's something implicating Taylor, it's probably gone already, but he was standing by the barn. It's a good idea to look. I'd rather not leave any stone unturned."

"Okay. We'll go there after," Henry agreed. "For now, I want to see where Barry died."

* * *

IN THE CENTER of the field knelt a petite woman, her hands clasped together in prayer. Her glasses perched on the end of her nose, and her lips appeared to move silently. Clad in a gingham dress and a white apron stained with dirt, she almost seemed like a character transported from another time.

"Virgie?" Henry asked. "Virgie, what are you doing out here?"

Virgie's eyes flew open, and she blinked away tears. "I can't believe it," she whispered brokenly. "Barry was such a wonderful man. He worked so hard here—he would fill in for me when I was feeling too ill to tend the fields. Did you know that? Now he's gone. I just..." Her voice cracked as she struggled to hold back her sobs.

Work the fields?

The skin on her hands was thin and mottled, with veins standing out like a road map. Her hair was wispy and silver, and her posture was slightly stooped. The woman kneeling in the dirt had to be at least seventy years old, if not more.

And she thought Barry Fields was a great guy for covering for her once in a while?

Henry stepped forward and put an arm

around Virgie's shoulders, offering her comfort. "I know it must be hard for you," he said. "Is this where Barry was killed, Virgie? Is that why you're at this spot?"

Well, Henry was turning out to be handy.

Virgie nodded and took a deep breath before continuing. "They found him here at this very spot. And Henry, I know that Scarlett was here last night—she comes around a lot these days now that we're getting old, but I don't think she had anything to do with this! In fact, I'm almost positive about it; I heard them talking last night, and they seemed happy! Her father frustrated her like any father, but she wouldn't have hurt him. She wouldn't have!"

Emma exchanged a glance with Henry before turning back to Virgie. "Do you know if anyone else came by around that time?" she asked.

Virgie looked at Emma with confusion.

"She's a police officer, Mrs. Curtis," Henry told her. "You can tell her."

"Well, now, this place is open to the public, ma'am. There are always people all over the place. People coming, people going, people working," Virgie replied. Then she hesitated, her expression troubled. "Except...there was one person who kept coming around asking all sorts of questions about what we did here at Strawberry Fields Farm. It was odd. Thomas Carmack." She looked up at Henry. "You must know him, Henry."

Henry nodded in agreement. "Yeah, I know him."

"Who is he?" Emma asked.

"He's been making the rounds around here lately, visiting a lot of family farms and asking too many questions," he explained. "He's trying to buy us out and drag us into his soulless corporate agriculture monstrosity, complete with pesticides and rows of crops placed too close together..."

"Wait a minute," Ami said, speaking up for the first time. "Are you talking about Carmack Foods?"

"That's him." Virgie frowned. "Seems like he was looking for something...or someone," she murmured, her gaze distant and thoughtful.

Emma looked between Henry and Virgie before speaking up again. "What did he say? I mean about who he was looking for."

Virgie shrugged her thin shoulders and reached up for Henry's outstretched hand to help her up. Her slight frame trembled under his grasp as she used his strong arm to stand. "I don't know, dear—he never said anything to me about any of that. All I know is that he kept asking about how much we produced and how many people worked here," she replied. "I didn't know. My memory's not what it used to be."

I kneeled down where Virgie said Barry Fields had taken his last breath and felt the cool, damp earth beneath my palm.

An image flashed in my mind—happiness about the warmth of the sun.

Beyond that?

Nothing.

Either the dirt that held the memory of what happened here had been removed with the body or—and this was, frankly, more likely—nature didn't care one whit about the death of one measly human in the middle of a strawberry field. The earth was surprisingly indifferent to the passing of seasons, whether its seasons or ours.

I scoured the ground with my eyes searching for the mysterious symbol Deputy Abernathy warned me about, but all I saw was the lush green grass, rich dirt, footprints and bootprints, and the jutting gray rocks dotting the ground.

CHAPTER SIX

$\mathcal{W}$e made our way back to the barn with Virgie Curtis trailing behind us, her shoulders shaking as she quietly wept.

Given that such symbols in the soil can be easily erased or trampled upon, it wasn't surprising that I couldn't spot any occult symbol at the crime scene. Presumably, the sheriff's office had taken a picture of the site before moving through it like a herd of elephants.

I just had to figure out how to get my hands on it.

"Tell me, Emma," I said, turning to my friend. "What do you know about Thomas Carmack?" Emma had been on the police force for years longer than I had been back in Forkbridge, and between that and her vampire brother Rex's club, I doubted there was a person in the area Emma didn't know or at least know of. "Would he kill someone to get his hands on a farm?"

Emma furrowed her brow in thought as we walked. "Not much more than Henry said, really. I know he's a wealthy businessman who's been trying to buy up a lot of local farms for some time now. But I don't know him personally, and I've never heard of him resorting to violence to get what he wants." She glanced at me. "People can surprise you, though. It's always possible he saw Barry Fields as an obstacle to his plans and took matters into his own hands."

I reached for my phone and sent a text to Althea, asking her to do some digging on Carmack's company. I knew she'd get back to me with any information she could find.

I held the text up to Emma so she could read it, and she nodded.

"I'm fine with Althea looking, but did you forget that Eddie used to be a detective?" Emma reminded me as we trailed behind the group. "I should give him a call and see if he can dig up some info for us. I mean, the guy's got a whole pack of werewolves at his beck and call to help with Hunter." She wrinkled her nose in distaste.

"Things not going well at the wolf den?"

Emma rolled her eyes. "You have no idea what it's like dating one guy and having four more come along for the ride. Four more that are sweet, generous, and caring—well, okay, except Lothian. He's just…Lothian. Though even he has his good points."

Lothian, who had been walking in front of us, turned and looked over his shoulder. "Thank you, my queen. You know I but live to serve your every whim."

Emma let out a deep sigh of frustration and scowled. She furrowed her brow and spoke through gritted teeth. "I'm stuck in a cheesy romance novel without the romance. Five men vying for my attention, but they're driving me crazy instead. It's like they're all on a mission to drive me up the wall." She gestured with her hands, emphasizing her point. "They're always around, hovering and watching my every move. I can't find a moment of peace or solitude. And on top of that, my house smells of cologne, aftershave, sweat, and baby poop. In that order. It's suffocating."

Wyatt glanced over his shoulder before increasing his pace, apparently intending to put as much distance between himself and Emma as possible.

Lothian, of course, did not.

"I don't know what to do. Look, they're all great guys. Honestly," Emma told me, her voice dropping lower. "But I did this in the military, you know? Living with a group of guys, existing where there was never a moment to myself, feeling like everyone could practically listen to every thought I had. I swear, Astra, the guys guarding me make me anxious. It's like I'm back in Afghanistan waiting for someone to attack." Emma's voice trailed off as the weight of her experience seemed to hang in the air between us. "At the beginning, I thought this might be fun."

"It's not fun?"

"It's not fun." She let out a heavy sigh and looked up at me, her eyes pleading for understanding. "I mean, Hunter's safe and well-protected, and I should be happy about that. But having five people constantly watching over us, it's suffocating." Emma's words tumbled out in a rush, her emotions getting the better of her. "I can't even take a step without one of them hovering over me, questioning my every move. It makes me feel like they don't trust me to take care of my own son."

"Oh, come on, Emma. That's not true. You know that."

Emma's face flushed with anger, and her voice rose in frustration. "And don't even get me started on the constant bickering and squabbling between them. It's like they're all trying to one-up each other, competing for who can be the most overbearing. Including Eddie." She shook her head, her hair falling in her eyes. "I appreciate their help, but I can't get a moment alone with the father of my kid. Sometimes it feels like too much."

"I hear you. You're a mother, but you're also a woman, and it has to be hard for you and Eddie to build a relationship with four other men around." I made eye contact with Emma. "You and Eddie need to find a way to build a relationship without always integrating the werewolf pack. Or Hunter, for that matter. I mean, you do want that, don't you?" Emma was quiet. "A romantic relationship with him?"

The silence went on too long.

"Emma?"

She looked up. "Look, I love Eddie. I loved him when we served together. I loved him when we reconnected. I love him even now when I want to send him on a week's vacation to get some quiet time with my kid. He's a great friend, and he knows every side of me. It's impossible not to love the guy."

"Then talk to him."

"If it was just Eddie, it wouldn't be a problem. We'd be able to work this out. I'm sure we could. I mean, I could at least explain my issues without feeling like a jerk." Emma lowered her gaze and picked at a loose thread on her sweater. "Love isn't the problem, Astra." She looked up again. "How do I tell him that part of who he is, the werewolf part, is driving me crazy? And it's not just him. My son is one of them. Don't I owe it to Hunter to find a way to integrate myself into this…this…this lifestyle? It's my responsibility—no, my obligation—to adjust. Isn't it?"

I didn't know what to say.

Goodness knows I was the last person to give human/paranormal relationship advice. My secret history wound up killing my boyfriend—though, to be fair, he didn't seem all that worse the wear for it.

"Emma, you have to talk to Eddie about this."

"Yeah," she said, her voice quivering with uncertainty. Emma tugged at her belt, her fingers tracing over the lump of her concealed weapon. She paused and gave a quick tap of assurance that it was still there and then forced a smile. "We're here, so let's put a pin in this. I'm just glad to be out of the house with only two werewolves attached to me instead of five."

Lothian walked ahead of us. I noticed the werewolf taking measured steps to maintain a safe distance that wouldn't suggest he was eavesdropping. And yet he made sure he stayed close enough to catch every word Emma and I exchanged.

Which kind of proved her point.

* * *

THE LARGE RED barn stood tall in the midday sunlight, its painted exterior radiating a bright and inviting hue. Inside, straw-covered wooden stalls filled the space, displaying colorful goods and offering activities for visitors. A number of tables were arranged around the perimeter, inviting people to talk and relax. The atmosphere remained still, as if waiting for the warm buzz of laughter and conversation to return.

Two sets of weathered wooden steps curved up the sides of the barn, each one leading to a pair of double doors that crowned the top. I glanced up, wondering what was on the second floor.

Everyone spread out and began looking for clues.

Except me.

I hurried to catch up with Lothian, but before I could speak, he turned to face me with a smug smirk on his lips as if he sensed me coming.

"Did you eavesdrop on our conversation?" I demanded, my voice tense.

He didn't answer, but the glint in his eyes told me everything I needed to know.

I let out a frustrated sigh. "Look, Lothian, I usually love a bit of sneakiness, but this time around, can you do me a favor and keep your mouth shut about what Emma and I were talking about?"

Lothian's laughter echoed off the walls. "You must be joking if you think I'd betray my allegiance to my werewolf alpha," he said, his tone dripping with sarcasm. "Come on, Astra, be serious. If Emma didn't want me to overhear, she wouldn't have said anything with me walking five steps ahead."

I clenched my fists, feeling my anger rise. Jeez, he was smug and annoying.

"Do you just not care about her pain? Is that it?" I shouted at him.

My voice reverberated through the empty barn, and I heard Emma's low, guttural moan of embarrassment coming from the direction of the pie stand.

Lothian's smug expression vanished in an instant. "Lower your voice," he cautioned me in a hushed tone.

"Listen, Pennington, we're not in high school anymore," I spat back, my words laced with disdain. "These are two adults who have a child together. Not everything is your concern or for your personal entertainment."

My words seemed to hit him like a slap in the face. His cheeks flushed with embarrassment or anger. I wasn't sure which.

Without warning, the werewolf grabbed my hand and pulled me toward the stairs. His touch was firm and unyielding, like an iron vice. "Upstairs," he said, pointing with his other hand. "You want to talk? Let's talk."

I didn't want to talk to him, I wanted to yell at him, but I followed Lothian up the stairs anyway. My feet pounded against the steps, the sound echoing through the barn.

As we climbed, I felt a wave of emotions wash over me, but…they weren't mine.

Lothian's worry for Emma was palpable, and it penetrated the barriers that Althea and I had established to shield against uninvited psychic visions whenever I made contact with people or objects. A series of vivid images flooded my mind. I saw Lothian pacing the hallway outside Emma's room, his face etched with anxiety as he listened to her muffled weeping from behind the door.

Huh.

At the top of the stairs, Lothian pushed open the set of double doors, revealing a large hallway filled with sunlight. The windows on the right side were open, and a gentle breeze wafted in, carrying the scent of cut grass and wildflowers.

The sound of our footsteps echoed off the walls as the werewolf dragged me deeper into the dimly lit corridor. I stole a quick glance at him, but his facial expression was a riddle I couldn't solve. After some time, he came to a stop about halfway down the corridor and turned to face me.

"What the hell are you doing?" I asked him. "You're lucky I didn't throw you down that flight of stairs that you just dragged me up."

"Look, Astra," he began, his voice low. "I know you're worried about Emma, and I get it. She's going through a tough time right now. But you have to understand I'm not going to betray my alpha. I'll listen to her, but I'm not going to keep things from him. Eddie needs to know what's going on, whether you like it or not."

"The hell he does! She told me that in confidence. She didn't tell you."

Lothian let out a deep sigh and raked his fingers through his tousled hair, his brow creased with worry. In a hushed tone, he finally broke the tense silence. "You do realize that Emma's well-being concerns more than you, right?" he said. "I'm as worried about her as you are."

My retort dripped with contempt as I spat out the words, "Well, it's only natural that you're 'concerned' about her. Eddie ordered you to be, didn't he? His commands always come first, even if it means disregarding the well-being of my friend."

"That's not fair—"

"Life's never been fair," I interjected, my voice acidic and dripping with venom. "You may stand outside her door and listen to her tears, but that doesn't mean you have the ability to actually do something about it."

Lothian's gaze flickered between his own outstretched hand and me. He balled it into a tight fist and then looked up, his expression one of disbelief. "You had the audacity to read me without my permission?"

"You grabbed me without my consent and then flooded my aura with your emotions while dragging me up the stairs like a brute," I said. The vibration of my phone against my hip was a distant, muffled sound that didn't distract me from my intense gaze into Lothian's eyes. "So don't you dare blame me for seeing what you shoved in my face. Psychically speaking," I added. "I saw what you showed me, and that's on you."

The werewolf averted his gaze, his expression inscrutable. "You're right," he conceded after a moment of silence. "I shouldn't have done that. I'm sorry."

"You fake guilt well. Why did you bring me up here?"

A faint smile tugged at the corners of his lips. "To talk."

"About Emma?" I asked.

He nodded. "And to apologize.

"For what?"

"I'm sorry if I sounded dismissive of your friend's feelings. Yes—I'm defensive about my pack. And yes, Emma is Hunter's mother, and I'm assigned to watch over her. But I also genuinely care about her," Lothian said, his voice softening. "It's tough to watch her and Eddie struggle so much. This should be the happiest time of their lives, and yet neither of them is happy."

I narrowed my eyes. "Really?"

"Yes. Really." He paused for a moment, searching my eyes for some hint of understanding. "I know you don't like me, Astra. And I know you don't trust me," he continued. "But I wish you would believe me when I tell you I'm not your enemy, nor Emma's. I want Eddie and Emma to be happy in whatever way they choose to be."

Lothian's voice was gentle, his words measured and imbued with a sense of honesty. I hesitated, unsure whether to believe him or not. "That was surprisingly sincere," I murmured, a hint of disbelief in my voice. "Or at least it sounded sincere."

"I'm not as heartless as you think," he said, his tone lighthearted.

"I wouldn't go that far," I replied, arching an eyebrow. "But I'll concede you may have slightly more heart than my current running assumption."

Lothian grinned, his eyes twinkling with amusement. "Well, that's something, I guess."

* * *

LOTHIAN'S LIPS pressed together as I reached for my phone, its noisy vibrations interrupting the silence between us for the third time. "One second, let me check this," I said before unlocking my phone and bringing up the latest text message.

It was from Emma.

BROCK COMING UPSTAIRS! HIDE NOW OR HE WILL SEE YOU!

My eyes widened as I read the message aloud to Lothian, and without hesitation, we both charged toward the "employees only" door. The two of us pushed past a large, heavy desk into the storage room packed with shelves. Every shelf, as far as the eye could see, was packed with jars of strawberry jam.

"There!" I whispered, pointing toward a large cabinet in a corner.

The big doors at the end of the hallway opened with a loud creak, and I heard heavy footsteps drawing closer. "There's a whole storeroom full of the stuff," a gruff voice called out. "As soon as they process the will and whatnot, I'll be able to get the recipe. Finally."

Two people?

I tried to count the footsteps.

Yup.

Two people.

Lothian and I huddled in the corner of the storeroom. We both inhaled sharply as two men stepped through the doorway into the room containing our hiding spot. We flattened ourselves against the wall, and I felt Lothian's heart racing next to mine. His scent filled the air around us—a mix of sandalwood and something slightly sweet that reminded me of cedar.

"Hey, Brock, thanks for the case of strawberry jam," one of them said. "The missus sure does like this stuff. Can't wait until I can get it any time I want it."

I peered around the corner, my nose almost touching the cool steel of the shelves, and squinted through the dimly lit room to catch a glimpse of the second man. He remained out of sight, concealed behind a towering stack of boxes.

Brock chuckled, his gravelly voice filling the room. "No problem at all. Fields really was obsessed with this stuff. He guarded the recipe like his life depended on it." He paused, his eyes scanning the room. "Maybe Johnson was so desperate to get it back that he killed Barry for it. Anything is possible in this cutthroat business, right?"

The two men laughed.

Cutthroat business, I thought.

Berry farms?

My quick intake of breath was too loud, and Lothian's grip on my arm tightened, urging me to stay quiet. I nodded, my eyes locked on the two men as they continued their conversation. The air was thick with tension, and the scent of strawberries and sandalwood lingered in my nostrils. It was almost overpowering in its sweetness.

Brock's hand slammed down on his friend's shoulder, causing an echoing thud to reverberate in the cramped storeroom. Finally, the two men exited the room, their footsteps heavy.

The way Brock Taylor acted was strange to me, given that his boss of almost twenty years had just been murdered the day before.

Neither of the men appeared to care a life had been taken.

Lothian's fingers curled and uncurled in the air as he spoke. "I couldn't see who the guy was that took the case of jam. Can you read the door or something?" he whispered, his voice barely audible in the tense silence.

I nodded, taking a deep breath before stepping forward toward the door. Placing my palm against the rough surface, I closed my eyes and focused on the energy within the room. A wave of sensations washed over me, like the subtle hum of a tuning fork. I let myself be pulled toward the strongest image—which was hopefully the most recent.

Got it.

I scrutinized the second man standing in front of my inner eye. He stood at least six feet tall, his frame lean and muscular. He was impeccably dressed in a tailored black suit that fit him like a glove, with a crisp white shirt and a black silk tie. In his hands, he held a silver clipboard, which he scanned with a disinterested air. The mystery man exuded an aura of confidence as if accustomed to being in charge.

However, his face remained hidden, obscured by his position facing away from the door. Over his shoulder on the clipboard, I could make out a corporate-looking logo with bold red letters that spelled out "CAH."

I opened my eyes and looked at Lothian. "I can't see his face, so I don't know who he is," I said. "But he had a clipboard clutched in his hand, and the emblem on it had the initials CAH."

Lothian's face contorted, and he arched an eyebrow. "Carmack Aggro Holdings," he muttered.

CHAPTER SEVEN

*L*othian and I crept down the hallway, carefully muffling our footsteps. Once outside, we made our way toward the rest of our team waiting by Johnson's large truck, past a towering stack of straw bales.

Emma was the first to speak. "Did he see you?"

"They, you mean?" I shook my head. "Nope, Brock Taylor and another person were inside, and the man who left with the case of jam was carrying a clipboard that read 'CAH.' So my guess is—"

"Carmack Aggro Holdings," Lothian said. "The parent company of Carmack Foods."

I looked at Henry Johnson to get his reaction to Lothian's announcement.

The farmer leaned against his truck, his muscular arms folded across his chest. His friendly demeanor remained unchanged, but his expression was hard to read. It was unclear to me whether he had any reaction to what Lothian had said.

"A case of jam?" Ami asked, confused.

"We hid in a storage room filled with case after case of strawberry jam. The two guys were chatting about it," Lothian explained. Turning to face Henry, she added, "Brock even implied that you might have killed Barry Fields for the recipe."

Henry's face remained placid as the outrageous allegation settled in the group, his hands clasped in front of him. "So, Thomas Carmack and Brock Taylor want to pin this on me, huh? Can't say I'm surprised to find the two of them working together, or that they'd try and find a way to get at my farm with this."

"Well, I mean, they said that," I said, "but honestly, they didn't seem too serious about the accusation."

Though Henry didn't know that a minute ago, I thought.

"Why would Thomas Carmack be here,

especially the day after Barry Fields was killed?" Emma's voice dripped with suspicion. "What's his connection to Brock Taylor?"

Henry shook his head. "Carmack wants to expand his corporate farming operations. Brock might inherit this place if he wins the court case and the inheritance. I guess Brock's already discussed the possibility of selling this farm."

Virgie's lip curled as she spoke. "Barry would never leave the farm to someone who would sell it to the likes of Thomas Carmack. He hated 'big food' and wanted to keep the land accessible to families for a wholesome day out. It was important to him, his way of addressing the issue of fatherlessness in the county."

Ami put her hand around Virgie and comforted the old woman while I tried to figure out how berry picking leads to fewer divorces in Central Florida.

"What a stand-up guy," I said with a touch of sarcasm.

Lothian's voice had a friendly quality as he addressed Henry. "So, that jam," he said. "What was so important about it that they believe you'd murder over it?"

Henry heaved a deep sigh and stuffed his hands into his pockets, avoiding Lothian's eyes.

Finally, after a moment of silence, he began his tale in a weary and bemused voice, as if he had repeatedly told the story.

"It all started with my great-great-grandad, William Johnson. Around the turn of the last century, people knew him as the best jam-maker in this part of the country. From blueberry to raspberry and everything in between, folks would travel for hours to get their hands on one jar made by him."

He paused to take a deep breath before continuing. "Like any smart person would do, Grandad kept the recipe close. He never shared it, wrote it down, or anything like that—or so the story goes. But as he got older, his mind started to slip, and eventually, he had to write it down to keep making it. That's when things took a turn for the worse."

Henry paused again and pointed down the road toward a cluster of trees. "See that place over there? That's where William built himself a cabin and storehouse. He kept all his supplies, including his special recipe ingredients and the recipe itself." It was a small clearing filled with thick undergrowth and a babbling stream. The sun glinted off the water's surface, sending shimmering flashes of light through the trees.

It was a peaceful place to put a cabin.

But there was no cabin.

"Someone stole it," Ami guessed.

"Not someone," Henry replied with a saddened smirk. "Josiah Fields lurked around the corners of my family's cabin until he broke the lock and snuck away with William's handwritten recipe for tart strawberry jam."

I raised an eyebrow. "Your great-great-grandfather couldn't remember any of the ingredients?"

"He could have. Maybe. But no one got a chance to ask him. Josiah Fields took the jam stores, the recipe, and lit the fire that reduced the cabin to ash. With my great-grandfather in it," he said as his gaze swept over the rolling hills of the farm. "Most of this used to be my family's. After the fire claimed my great-great-grandfather's life? My great-great-grandmother sold it for a pittance. One week after the sale, Josiah Fields became an overnight success selling jam made from a recipe he stole from my family. On land he may as well have stolen. Or so the story goes."

"That's horrible," Virgie said.

"Awful," Ami agreed.

Henry shrugged. "For them, sure. Tragic. But

for me? It's history. It was over a hundred years ago."

"That's why," Lothian asked, "they thought you killed Barry Fields for the recipe? Because of something that happened a hundred years ago?"

Henry nodded. "I suppose so," he said, "but I didn't do it. I know what happened haunted my grandfather a little bit. He used to talk about that jam recipe like it had magic fairy dust, but we got other land. We rebuilt down the road from this place. My father and Barry Fields made a deal where we'd help them with distribution. It's all water under the bridge."

We all stood there in silence, contemplating Henry's story.

"To be clear," he added, "I don't know why they would think I had anything to do with Barry's murder. I'm not killing someone over a hundred-year-old jam recipe theft. It was a long time ago. That history isn't relevant anymore."

* * *

HISTORY HAS a way of making its own decisions about what is relevant and what isn't, choosing what is meant to be remembered and what is meant to be forgotten. The secrets of the past had a way of resurfacing and striking back at those who dismissed them too easily.

My mother was the perfect example.

A reminder that things happening in the shadows are never invisible forever.

Emma's voice broke through my reverie, "What's going on in that head of yours?"

"Nothing." I gazed down at the grove of trees below us. "I just wonder what secrets those trees are keeping."

Emma raised a skeptical brow. "Seriously? You think this century-old crime will shed light on what's happening now?"

Emma had a point—we had been wandering around this farm for hours, yet all we had to show for it was the connection between Brock and Thomas Carmack and the Fields and Johnson farms; otherwise, the search had been fruitless.

Well, except for Henry Johnson himself.

Oh, and the story of the great strawberry jam theft. Strawberry jam was made of fruit.

So, not fruitless.

I spotted Archie's bright eyes staring at us as he descended from the treetops. I stepped back when he jolted and screeched, his wings fanning out around him as he spotted Henry. He hovered briefly before banking to the left and shooting back into the sky, soaring away from us and back toward the tree line.

Oops.

Henry fixed his eyes on Archie's retreat. "Wow, that angry owl almost landed on your head! That was insane."

"Yeah, lucky me," I said, wiping my brow.

Lothian, Wyatt, Ami, and Emma exchanged knowing looks, amused by my attempt to act like I hadn't known the large owl dive-bombing me. I scratched the back of my head, trying to appear nonchalant.

"Definitely wild to see an owl so close," Henry replied. Archie was a blur of motion until he vanished within the leaves, and Henry kept staring up at the canopy of branches. "I wonder what he thought you were."

Virgie stepped closer to us and looked up toward the canopy. "I didn't know we had owls like that at the farm," she said. "There are usually little brown barn owls around here. They don't usually get that big or fly close like that one did."

"I'm pretty sure there are lots of owls like that around here," Henry told her. "That one wasn't unique, really. As far as owls go."

I was glad Archie wasn't close enough to hear what Henry said.

Virgie's gaze dropped to the ground, her face crumpling as fresh tears rolled down her cheeks. "My momma said that when someone you love passes away, their spirit will return to you as a bird," she whispered, lifting her eyes skyward. "I wonder if that's Barry come to make sure we're all right."

The bird was definitely not Barry Fields, but I couldn't bring myself to tell the grieving woman that her mother's tall tale was nothing more than that. Our deceased kin didn't come back in the form of a bird to watch over us.

They haunted us in the shadows and reflections.

"Do you think it's time to go see Scarlett in jail?" I asked Emma. I had grown tired of the existential avian discussion on the afterlife and was ready to leave. "We've run out of stuff to do here. I think it's time to talk to the accused murderer and see what she says."

Out of the corner of my eye, I saw Henry's face twist in discomfort at the mention of Scarlett's name.

Huh.

What was that about?

The friendly farmer seemed to be fighting the urge to shrink away from the conversation, his discomfort clear to anyone who saw him. Henry shifted his gaze away from the group as if searching for an escape from the conversation.

Huh.

Was that guilt I saw on his face?

Maybe friendly Henry wasn't so innocent after all.

Ami objected to the jail side trip. "I don't see why we need to talk to her anyway. We already know she's innocent. Why waste our time before we have information that can help her? I'd hate for her to get her hopes up for nothing."

Emma shook his head and sighed. "It's not that simple, Ami. We need to find out what she knows. There might be something we're missing." She turned to Henry. "Can we call on you to get back on this property? I'd rather come back without a warrant if I can manage it."

Can police on maternity leave get warrants?

Asking for a friend.

I glanced at Henry again, wondering if he knew more than he was letting on. His eyes caught mine and then shifted away as if avoiding my gaze.

I couldn't tell if his discomfort resulted from guilt or something else.

And I didn't like that I couldn't tell.

"I'm happy to help in any way I can," Henry told her, the offer kind even as his voice seemed edged with something else. "Give me about an hour's notice, and I'll do my best to get away." Henry immediately entered his number after Emma handed him her phone.

It all seemed fine. He seemed fine.

But I couldn't shake the feeling that something was off about him.

Unfortunately, I didn't have time to dwell on it.

* * *

UNTIL I WAS in the car driving.

Then I could dwell.

We said our goodbyes and climbed back into the Jeep, with Lothian and Wyatt trailing us on their motorcycles. As I drove toward the county jail, my mind kept returning to Henry Johnson and his peculiar behavior toward the end of our conversation. I tried to shake the feeling that he was hiding something, but it persisted, nagging at me.

Was it a connection to the Carmacks?

The Fields family?

Did the stolen recipe and arson a hundred years ago mean something despite what he said?

Or was it something else?

Driving didn't give me the relief or pleasure that it usually did. My mind was full of a nagging feeling that I'd missed something about Henry. Something obvious, but something just out of my reach.

"Why didn't you shake his hand goodbye?" Emma asked.

"What?" I asked her, barely registering the sight of the jail in the distance, its imposing walls contrasting with the otherwise peaceful landscape.

"Your expression tells me that you're as bothered as I am by Henry's reaction when I mentioned Scarlett," Emma said. "I saw it too, and I'm curious why you didn't grab Farmer Jeb's hand and shake it if it's driving you this crazy trying to figure it out."

"I don't know what you're talking about."

"Oh, you are such a liar." She pointed to the driveway and said, "Pull in over there."

As we drove into the parking lot, I couldn't help but notice the high chain-link fence that enclosed the area. It was a monolith of cinder block and razor wire standing sentry against the idyllic surroundings. The uninviting building blended into the background of the grassy fields and winding country roads.

I parked the Jeep and said, "It never even occurred to me to read Henry's thoughts without permission. I assumed he wasn't a suspect." As I recalled Lothian's angry reaction when I had done the same to him, I added, "I have ethics, you know, Emma."

"Oh, dear lord." Emma's lips curled into a smirk as she reached for the door handle. "Everyone's always a suspect," she said, her voice taking on a menacing tone. "So, that was your first mistake. Haven't I taught you anything?"

We stepped out of the Jeep, and the sun-baked asphalt radiated heat from the parking lot. "You know, you should become a detective full-time after your maternity leave."

"Har har, very funny," Emma replied, stopping to check the time on her wristwatch. "Oh no, visiting hours are almost over. Only two of us can go in for half an hour, and there are five of us." She looked around at our small group. "So, who's going in?"

"You and Astra, I guess?" Ami suggested. "You guys were partners, so it makes sense. That, and you know Scarlett better than we do."

"Right." Emma crossed her arms and furrowed her eyebrows, her lips pressed together in deep concentration.

"If I'm right, why do you look like that?" my sister asked Emma.

"Because what you said? That's not positive." Emma sighed and rubbed the back of her neck. "Yeah, here's the deal— I'm a small-town detective, and this is a big county jail. If you didn't sense it from Abernathy's obvious contempt for me, they think they're superior. The other point? It's common knowledge that detectives should avoid interrogating someone they know on a personal level. I could sway the conversation and cloud the truth." Emma looked at Ami. "You could, too, for that matter. You're sure she's innocent because your cards told you so."

"She is innocent."

"See?"

"No." Ami frowned. "Why is that bad?"

"Because that's a potential conflict of interest."

"Who should go in, then?" Wyatt asked.

"Well, Astra already suspects that very nice Henry Johnson—even though he helped us out. And he assisted us in running all over the Strawberry Fields Farm looking for clues," Emma pointed out. She moved under a nearby tree seeking respite from the scorching sun as we decided who would go in. "I don't think your tarot cards or my previous dealings with Scarlett will make a dent in her opinion."

"And that's a good thing?"

Emma nodded. "I know it doesn't sound like it, but yes." She turned her gaze toward Lothian, standing tall and proud beneath the sizzling sun. "I don't think Lothian has any capacity for emotion or any agenda that doesn't involve his interests alone," she mused, her eyes hardening. "So I guess he's not a bad choice to send with her."

A sly smirk revealed itself on Lothian's lips. "You make me sound like a heartless sociopath, my queen," he chuckled in a way that suggested he was only partially joking.

Emma's lips curved up in a cold smirk. "If the diagnosis fits."

I handed the keys to Emma so that Ami, Emma, and Wyatt could escape the sweltering sun and relax in the cool interior of the car. Emma nodded and motioned for the rest to follow her.

Lothian and I walked toward the towering building in front of us, its walls made of thick metal bars that seemed to stretch forever. As we approached the door, I couldn't help but notice the sign that declared, "Visitors must be escorted by an officer at all times," as if this was Alcatraz.

"Cheerful," I muttered as Lothian held the door open for me.

"Try not to touch anything," he said, his voice low. "I imagine the emotions soaking these walls and the memories you'd find are rather unpleasant."

I nodded.

Lothian was right.

And I didn't even get annoyed by his suggestion.

Great.

The ominous atmosphere of the building was already getting to me. I couldn't help but feel uneasy about what we would find inside.

CHAPTER EIGHT

Taking a deep breath, I stepped inside the county jail and felt the chill of the air conditioning hit my skin. Lothian walked in behind me, close enough that I could feel the warmth of his werewolf body but far enough back that he didn't crowd me.

Werewolves put out a lot of heat.

That was one thing Twilight got right.

The room felt cold and sterile, its concrete walls painted again with a dull, spiritless gun metal gray.

The county must have bought the paint in bulk.

A high gloss made the linoleum floor shine, but it only accentuated the lifelessness of the space. Against one wall, they'd bolted a row of metal chairs to the ground, even though this was nothing more than a lobby.

The overpowering smell of disinfectant did little to cover up the underlying odor of sweat and despair.

We stood before a long, imposing counter manned by a bored-looking guard. His eyes flicked over us before returning to his computer screen.

Rude.

The atmosphere was oppressive, and I couldn't wait to leave.

The guard behind the counter—Roland Ball— jerked his eyes back at me, his eyes widening in surprise before narrowing into a sneer. I could feel Lothian tense up behind me, his protective instincts kicking in at the slightest hint of hostility.

I put on my best smile and tilted my head to the side as I addressed the sour guard. "Good afternoon," I said. "We'd like to visit with Scarlett Fields today. Could you please point us in the right direction?"

An insidious expression flickered across the guard's face, a mix of revulsion and something else, something sinister and harder to define. It made me uneasy, and I couldn't shake the feeling that there was more going on here than met the eye. "How do you know her?"

"I don't believe we need to tell you that," Lothian responded smoothly.

The guard stared.

Lothian stared back.

The clock on the wall ticked loudly.

The guard, who had been eyeing us with a mixture of curiosity and thinly veiled hostility, finally broke his silence. "You're wasting your time, anyway," he drawled, casting a dismissive glance in our direction. He raised his hand and brushed his unruly hair out of his eyes, revealing a set of small burns on his fingers and palms. As he caught my gaze, he quickly lowered his hand, looking away as if to hide the marks from my view.

"Those look like they hurt."

"I'm a glass blower at the local Ren Fair," he blurted out, as if trying to preempt any further questions. "Anyway, Scarlett's guilty as sin. My best friend knows her from the farm. Her and her father? Fought all the time. She was a wild one. My ex-girlfriend always said." He sneered, his voice dripping with contempt. "She deserves to be in a cage."

I looked at his name tag—C.O. Roland Ball.

Officer Roland Ball had a lot of opinions.

Lothian stepped forward, his voice low and dangerous. "I don't see how her guilt or innocence is relevant to her visitation privileges," he said. "Even guilty people are allowed visitation. Are you able to help us with that, or not?"

Officer Ball narrowed his eyes at us but seemed to think better of pushing the issue. "Yeah, whatever." He gave us the information we needed, and we made our way through the sterile halls of the jail, heading toward the visiting area.

The hallway was lit by cold, blue-tinted LED bulbs, casting an eerie glow over everything. The gun metal gray walls seemed to loom over us as if closing in on all sides, and as we walked, the sound of our footsteps echoed off the walls. It was like we were lost in some endless, labyrinthine maze.

"I hate it here," I muttered.

"I don't think you're supposed to like it here."

Lothian's words only served to irritate me further. "Wow, really? Thanks for the insight," I shot back. I gave him a withering glance before returning my focus to the endless hallway ahead.

My heart sank when we finally arrived at the

visiting room, which was as bleak and lifeless as the rest of the jail. The space was filled with rows of tables, each one bolted to the ground. The metal chairs were hard and uncomfortable, with no padding or cushioning to soften their unforgiving surfaces.

They had placed plastic dividers between each table, creating an illusion of privacy that was shattered by the presence of other visitors. It was hard to imagine any visitors or inmates being able to find any sense of comfort or solace in this space.

Scarlett was already seated at a table, her wrist handcuffed to a metal loop.

A female guard nodded at us and pointed to Scarlett's table. As we approached, I couldn't help but feel a wave of gratitude that Emma didn't experience the harsh reality of her friend in this place. Scarlett looked utterly lost and defeated, her eyes downcast as if she couldn't bear to meet our gaze.

"Scarlett," I said once we sat down across from her. "How are you holding up?"

She looked up, her eyes filled with a haunted sadness that made my heart ache. "I'm not," she said. "I'm not holding up at all. My father's dead, Astra. Dad and I had our differences, that's for sure. He never understood me, but all parents have trouble understanding their kids, right?" Scarlett swallowed. "He's dead, and it's all my fault."

Her fault?

Lothian cleared his throat. "Before we get into that, are you doing okay in here? Do you need anything?"

Scarlett shrugged. "I'm fine," she said, but her eyes told a different story. There was a tiredness there, a weariness that spoke of a lonely, sad night without sleep. "It's not great," she added and then shrugged again. "It's not exactly the Ritz here, but I'm managing. This creepy kid I went to high school with is a guard, so that's nuts. Small towns, right? But I have a lawyer. I talked to him on the phone and I'm sure he'll get around to seeing me. Eventually."

I nodded, glancing around the room. It was crowded, with several other visitors talking in hushed tones to their loved ones on the other side of the plexiglass dividers. The sound of their voices was a low murmur, like the distant hum of a beehive.

"How's your case going?" I asked, turning back to Scarlett.

She sighed. "Not great. I talked to Joe Banning

on the phone. My lawyer? He said they've got a lot of evidence against me. But I don't see how that's possible. I didn't do it. If I didn't do it, how could there be evidence against me?"

I didn't answer her. "What did you mean when you said your father's death was your fault?"

Scarlett leaned back in her seat, her eyes closing for a moment. When she opened them, they were filled with tears. "I was the last person to see him alive," she said, her voice barely above a whisper. "We had a fight, a bad one. I said some things I didn't mean. He stormed out of the house, and I didn't try to stop him. I thought he'd come back, but he never did. If we hadn't been fighting, he would have stayed in the house and never been in the strawberry patch last night."

Lothian leaned forward, his eyes fixed on Scarlett. "What was the fight about?"

"Thomas Carmack," she said and made a face. "Someone told Dad that Carmack had been coming around the farm to talk to me, but that's not true. I'd never give that jerk the time of day. Dad was furious that I was talking to him, but I wasn't!"

* * *

LOTHIAN TOOK charge of the interrogation then, asking Scarlett to start from the beginning. "What happened after your father left the house?" he asked.

Scarlett shook her head. "I don't know. Dad left, and I went up to my room to go to bed. The next thing I knew, the police were banging on my door, saying they had found my father's body a mile away from the house. Right next to an occult sigil. They told me I'd been seen running from there by a witness, but that's impossible. I was in bed."

Lothian leaned forward in his chair. "Did they say how he died?"

"Hit in the head with something. They didn't say what."

Blunt force trauma, then. Given his age, even a rugged farmer like him would have difficulty fighting off an attacker once they landed a solid blow to the head.

I watched Scarlett. I noted the subtle shifts in her expressions as she spoke of her father's murder. Her reactions, the flashes of pain—all of it seemed genuine. I tried to detect any hint of deception or dishonesty.

But I found none.

"How did they know the symbol they found at

the scene was an occult sigil?" I asked her. "A sigil for what? What was its purpose?"

"I have no idea!" Scarlett said. "I didn't know what it was. The police claimed it was some kind of magic symbol, but it didn't match any of the ones I'd studied. The lines and circles were all haphazard without any logic or meaning I could see." She went on to explain that she'd seen a photo of it. It was etched into the dirt next to her father's hip and looked like someone had used a stick or a branch to create it. "The dirt around it was weird, too, like someone had knelt down. They took my pants to look for dirt, but I work on a farm. Of course they'll find dirt."

I pulled out a small pad and a pen. "Can you draw it for me?"

Scarlett nodded and took the pen and paper from me. She started to draw the sigil, her hand shaking. As she drew, I noticed she was biting her lower lip as if trying to hold back tears. When Scarlett finished drawing, she handed the paper back to me. "That's not perfect, but it's pretty close," she told me.

I studied the sigil for a moment, trying to find any meaning or significance in its lines and circles. But, like Scarlett, I couldn't make heads or tails of it. "Can I keep this?" I asked her.

She nodded, and I folded the paper and slipped it into my pocket.

Lothian spoke up again. "Did your father have any enemies, Scarlett? Anyone who might want to hurt him?"

Scarlett shook her head. "No, not that I know of. He was a good man, well-liked in the community. He didn't have any enemies that I can think of." She shifted in her seat. "I know I complained at the Farmers' Market about him that day, but Dad always meant well. He didn't have any sons, and after Mom died in the car accident, he just... changed. Tried to protect me too much, you know?"

Protect?

Scarlett was being generous.

As I thought back to my encounter with Barry Fields on the day of his death, I couldn't feel the same as Scarlett. Sure, he seemed like a nice enough person, and even Emma, who was as harsh a judge of character as I'd ever met, had a fondness for the old man. But his words had revealed something else, too—a deep-seated misogyny that left a bad taste in my mouth.

As a woman who worked in a male-dominated field, I knew all too well the impact that even "nice" misogyny could have. It wasn't just about the blatant discrimination or harassment. It was about the little things, the unconscious biases and assumptions that could add up to impact our careers and lives over time.

I saw it in how some of my male colleagues would talk over me in meetings or assume that I wasn't interested in the technical aspects of a military mission. They didn't mean any harm— they were nice guys, after all—but their behavior still reinforced the idea that women were somehow less capable or competent than men.

And then there were the more overt examples of misogyny, like the coworker who told me I was "too pretty" to be a good soldier.

I wasn't too pretty to sweep his legs and lay him out.

But that's a story for another time.

Barry Fields' attitudes toward Emma for being an unmarried mother and his daughter for wanting to run the farm without a husband all pointed to deep-seated misogyny. While that misogyny may not have had anything to do with his death, it was still a piece of the puzzle that nagged at me, just like Henry Johnson's reaction to Scarlett's name nagged at me.

"Scarlett, I promise we'll do everything we can to find out who did this to your father," I said, sounding as reassuring as possible. "Emma's with me, out in the parking lot. We're both committed to getting to the bottom of this. In the meantime, is there anyone else we can talk to? Anyone who might have seen something that day?"

Henry Johnson, I thought. Say Henry Johnson.

Scarlett bit her lip, lost in thought. "Well, someone came up to Dad's booth right before he got all mad and picked a fight with me," she said. "I didn't see who it was, but they were talking to him for a few minutes. Maybe Dad said something to them?"

"Do you remember what they looked like?" Lothian asked.

Scarlett shook her head. "It was a guy about Dad's height. He was wearing a navy blue jacket with yellow stripes on it. The stripes were running down the sides of his arm from the shoulder. Like this?" Scarlett touched her shoulder and dragged her fingers down her arm to demonstrate. "I remember thinking he stood so straight and had his hands clasped behind his back, too. Kind of like a sailor or military guy."

The guard's voice echoed through the bleak visiting room, announcing that our time was up. I felt a sense of frustration and disappointment.

We had made some progress, but it still felt like we were missing a vital piece of the puzzle.

"We'll keep looking into this, Scarlett," I promised as we rose from our seats. "And we'll keep you updated on any new developments. Call Emma collect if you think of anything. And hang in there."

* * *

LOTHIAN and I followed the guards out of the visiting room. As we made our way back down the dimly lit hallways of the jail, I couldn't help but look back over my shoulder. There, by the door to the cells, stood Scarlett in chains, looking small and alone.

Lothian's question caught me off guard as we walked through the jail halls. "Can I ask you something?" he said, his voice low and serious.

"Sure," I replied, bracing myself for whatever he might throw my way.

"Why didn't you grab Scarlett's hand and read her thoughts?" he asked, his eyes searching my face for a reaction. "There were no bars between Scarlett and us. It might have helped us if you had seen the guy's jacket firsthand. Or his hair or height."

I took a moment to gather my thoughts before responding. "Sure, I could have done that," I said, "but it's not that simple. My power doesn't work like a remote control. I can't pick and choose what I want to see. Each energy signature or person has its strongest memory, which is not always the one I want. Sometimes it's a traumatic event that's seared into their mind, something they're haunted by, or some recollection that's taken over."

Lothian looked at me as we walked, waiting for me to continue.

"If I had grabbed Scarlett's hand," I said, "what do you think I would have seen? The guy in the jacket? Maybe. But more likely, it would have been something else, something she's been carrying with her for years. Or some recent trauma like—"

"—the police busting down her door telling her that her father's been murdered, and she's going to jail," he finished, sighing.

I nodded. "Yep."

Lothian glanced at me, his expression thoughtful. "I understand. And even if you had seen the guy in the jacket," he said, "it wouldn't be enough to identify him. She didn't see his face."

"Exactly."

"You said you don't always get what you want," he said, his eyes searching my face. "Does that mean you sometimes see something you don't want to see?"

Well, obviously, I thought.

"If I touch a person—or an animal, something with a mind—intending to read their memories, I will get an image of something. It might be the last thing they were thinking of. It might be their happiest memory. It might be a memory that the person thinks they've blocked out, but that's still in their subconscious."

Lothian's gaze bore into me. "But sometimes," he asked, "it's something worse?

"Sometimes," I said.

"Like what?"

"I don't like to talk about it much," I admitted. "Suffice it to say, my gift is most useful when someone's done something wrong and feels guilty about it. When someone feels guilty about doing something terrible, it's all they can think about. Even if I wanted to see something different, they wouldn't let me. All they can do is subconsciously shove their crime in my face."

Our steps echoed off the walls of the empty hallway like whispers until we reached the end of the corridor and saw the exit sign just ahead.

"Well, that's pretty undisciplined."

"Most criminals aren't sociopathic masterminds like you," I said. "They're people faced with something tempting that looked easy, and they jumped on it in a moment of weakness. They just failed to uphold their own morality." I smiled at the werewolf. "Unlike you, who has no morality."

Lothian stepped in front of me, blocking my exit, and turned to face me with a sly grin. "You really don't like me, do you?" he asked. "I like you, you know. You're a fascinating witch."

Was I supposed to thank him?

"I never said I didn't like you," I told him.

"Aha!" Lothian's eyes widened in amusement. "So you like me?" he pressed.

"Don't get ahead of yourself," I replied, sounding nonchalant. "I never said I liked you." His teasing banter was oddly charming and reminded me of my military life. "Are you going to move out of my way, or should I book a cell?"

Lothian's cocky smile widened. "You like me," he said, pushing open the door with his back and stepping backward out of the building. "You don't want to admit it, but you like me."

I rolled my eyes and followed him outside, trying not to let his teasing affect me. Deep down,

I couldn't deny that something about him drew me in. Maybe it was his confident swagger or the danger that seemed to surround him like a cloak.

Whatever it was, I knew I needed to be careful not to get sucked in by it.

Lothian was a werewolf, after all.

Werewolves exuded sex appeal.

They just did.

As we stepped out into the warm Florida sun, I felt a sense of relief. Being inside the jail was suffocating, and the fresh air was a welcome change. Lothian turned to me, his eyes scanning my face.

"Well, I like you, Astra," he said, his tone serious. "You see me for who I am and still like me. That's pretty rare for a guy like me."

"You hear what you want to hear. I never said I liked you."

The werewolf's eyes scanned my face. "Yeah, I know. But you do."

I really wanted to punch him in the face.

He was just so cocky.

Unbearably so.

Unbelievably so.

Even without that patronizing grin on his handsome face, he exuded an air of narcissistic conceit that made my skin crawl.

Without warning, I gave him a gentle jab in the ribs that made him gasp and let out a muffled laugh as he coughed. "Some advice for you, Fido. Never tell a woman how she feels."

"Yes, ma'am," Lothian responded with a grin.

CHAPTER NINE

"*E*mma!" Ayla shouted, and Cerberus barked in response as she spotted us walking into Arden House. "Did you bring Hunter?"

"Of course not," Emma replied as we walked into Arden House. "Hunter's an infant. He's not old enough to investigate murders yet. He's still in diapers. We can let him take a crack at a burglary, but no way he should be investigating murders. Not until he's at least a year."

Althea stood at the end of the dimly lit hallway, the flickering light from the candles casting eerie shadows on the walls. Her sleek laptop was securely tucked under one arm, and her strikingly iridescent black-feathered crow,

Lily, perched on her other arm just below her shoulder. Her face was etched with concern, her furrowed brow and tightened lips reflecting the tension she felt. Althea's foot tapped impatiently against the polished hardwood floor, creating a sharp staccato sound that reverberated down the corridor.

"You got something?" I asked.

"Carmack Aggro Holdings?" Her voice dripped with disdain, and her upper lip curled in disgust. "It's a despicable company, run by an even more despicable little man. I'm not talking about Thomas, though. Have you heard of Gordon Carmack? He's a cutthroat businessman, a real snake." Lily scurried up her arm and perched on top of her head. "He's Thomas's father and a truly nasty piece of work."

"I haven't, so tell me. What's so bad about the company?"

Althea was my go to person when digging up dirt on people; she was never a disappointment. Her eyes glittered with excitement as she launched into her explanation.

"Well, for starters, they've been caught dumping pesticides and fertilizers into the rivers near their factory farms more than once. More than one river, more than one farm, more than one time. A lot more than once," she began, her words tumbling out in a rush. "And they've been sued for unfair labor practices, discrimination against women, the disabled, minorities. They have a history of bribing government officials to look the other way."

"Well, this company sounds just fantastic," Ami said sarcastically.

"The damage they cause from their industrialized agriculture practices is awful. Just awful." Althea's voice was a mix of contempt and outrage, and her eyes were full of simmering indignation. "They place profit above the health of consumers, the environment, animals—they care about money. That's it. And they're unapologetic about it. I think I'm a vegetarian now after reading all that."

"Isn't that basically every single big food corporation, though?" Emma asked.

"No," Althea told her. "This is next level. The damage they cause is inexcusable; it's greed to the point of recklessness. They have zero regard for the well-being of anyone, anything—money is all that matters to them, and they couldn't care less who they harm."

"Why do they want to buy these small farms?" I asked her. "I can't believe Strawberry Fields

Farms is taking a huge market share from the Carmacks."

Althea's face twisted into a scowl. "Humane washing," she seethed.

"Humane washing," Lothian repeated. "What's that?"

"A tactic to make the Carmacks brands appear more ethical than they actually are. They want to use the Strawberry Fields Farms name to make themselves appear more ethical," my sister explained, her dark eyes flashing. "It's all smoke and mirrors. Those small places look like paradise for the animals, for the workers. But those places are nothing but a show. The food doesn't come from those farms at all. They want to use it as a brand to make themselves look good."

"So, they buy out smaller, more humane companies and use their branding to give the illusion of ethical practices? That's dishonest. And disgusting," Ami said, her eyes wide with disbelief.

Cerberus growled at her feet as if to agree.

I arched an eyebrow, fixing my gaze on Althea. "You're basically suggesting that these guys are perfectly capable of brutally bashing an elderly man and leaving him to die in a strawberry patch to get a farm if they wanted it?"

"I'm saying these people would kick a puppy if someone paid them a nickel."

With a flurry of fluttering wings, Archie sailed through the backyard's French doors and landed on a perch near the ceiling. He looked down at us. "Are you people just going to stand in the hallway?" he asked. Archie glided down from his perch and landed on the counter. "The kitchen is better. There's bacon in the kitchen."

The bulldog's ears perked up at the mention of bacon, and he bounded off toward the kitchen with a happy bark. His nose twitched with excitement and anticipation.

"It's almost dinner time," Ayla called after Cerberus, but the dog didn't seem to care. "We're going to sit down and eat soon."

"That doesn't preclude anything I said, right?" The owl stretched out his wings and ruffled his feathers, then turned his head to fix Ayla with a piercing stare. "What's wrong with bacon for dinner? Nothing. There's nothing wrong with bacon for dinner."

Cerberus barked eagerly from the floor as Aunt Gwennie bustled into the room from the laundry area. "Emma, are you and the wolves staying to eat?" she asked as she uncovered a pot on the stove and peeked in. "It's not bacon, but I think everyone will enjoy it just as much. I'm making meatballs and stuffed ravioli."

"Is it stuffed with bacon?" Archie asked. He couldn't frown, per se, but he would have been if he could.

Emma smiled at Aunt Gwennie. "I'm sure it'll be delicious."

"I'm not sure if that's a yes or a no on the bacon," Archie told her.

"Or a yes or a no on staying for dinner," Aunt Gwennie added.

Emma craned her neck to look up at Lothian and Wyatt, the towering figures flanking her on either side. With their bulging muscles and crossed arms, they looked like imposing sentinels, ready to pounce at any moment. It was hard not to laugh at the absurdity of it all.

"I know I should probably get back," she sighed, "but it's nice to have a change of scenery. This is the longest I've been away from the house since Hunter was born. It's nice to have a moment to think."

It wasn't the longest she'd been out of the house since the baby.

It was, however, the longest she'd been away from Eddie and Hunter.

* * *

WE SETTLED into the warm and inviting dining area, the comfortable chairs and soft lighting creating a sense of ease and relaxation. As we gazed out through the open back door, the fiery orange sun sank below the horizon, casting a warm glow across the room.

Aunt Gwennie brought out the food, and Ayla immediately jumped up to help serve. "I have fresh Parmesan like you get in the restaurants." She held up a wedge of hard cheese and a grater. "It's way better than that store-bought stuff."

"Wait, where's the bacon?" Archie said, his head swiveling frantically.

"No bacon tonight, I'm sorry to say," Aunt Gwennie said, shaking her head.

Cerberus whined.

"That's a shame," Archie said. He swooped from his perch at the edge of the table and snagged a meatball from the serving tray with his beak, but before he got a few feet with it, it dropped. Cerberus leaped up and grabbed the meatball in mid-air.

As we chatted and laughed over our plates, the worries and stresses of the day melted away, replaced by a sense of camaraderie and contentment. The simple pleasures of good food and good company were all we needed to lift our spirits and find a moment of peace.

As we savored the last few bites of the delicious meal, Ayla's smile faded, and her gaze drifted toward Emma. "So, we know what we found here. What happened at the farm today?" she asked, her voice tinged with concern.

Aunt Gwennie's brow furrowed as if she disapproved of discussing work at the dinner table.

As Emma began to speak, the room grew quieter, the low hum of the night bugs outside adding to the tense atmosphere. The darkness of the approaching night enveloped us, casting long shadows across the room.

We listened as Emma recounted our experiences. She described the unexpected arrival of Henry Johnson, the chaos of me and the werewolf stuck in the jam storeroom, and the chance discovery of Carmack and Taylor's connection as Lothian and I hid in the shadows.

"So, you still don't think Scarlett Fields

committed the murder?" Wyatt finally said, breaking the silence.

Ami scoffed at the suggestion, rolling her eyes. "Of course she didn't," she said. "My tarot reading made it clear that she's innocent."

I shook my head. "Tarot readings aren't always right. Even if we assume they are, interpretations can be wrong. We can't move forward in a case based on a tarot reading. We still have to investigate."

Lothian shook his head, his expression skeptical. "I agree with Astra," he admitted. "I think we need to rely on solid evidence and facts."

Ayla glared at me, her eyes narrowing with anger. "I forgot, only your magic is perfect," she said, her voice dripping with sarcasm and a hint of bitterness. "The rest of us are fallible."

"I never said I was perfect," I replied, calm but firm. "I try to do my best, like everyone else."

Aunt Gwennie leaned in, her voice low and commanding. "Now, you girls have been doing a great job of not tearing into one another lately," she said firmly, her eyes darting back and forth between us. "But I don't want to see any backsliding here. I don't have enough headache medicine to deal with your bad attitudes."

Althea clenched her jaw and pinched the bridge of her nose, her frustration evident. She glared at Ayla. "I know you're upset about not getting to go on the murder field trip," she said, her voice measured but stern. "But that's no excuse for being rude. Astra didn't deserve that."

Ayla's expression softened, and she looked down at her lap, clearly ashamed of her behavior. "I'm sorry," she muttered. "It was childish of me."

Althea nodded, her expression softening. "I understand how you feel," she said, her voice gentler now. "But we're a team, and we have to work together if we're going to solve this case."

"Hey, I barely got to go either, kid," Archie told her, his tone irritated. "They had humans with them almost the whole day, and every time I tried to come down out of the trees, there was someone with a cell phone. Probably with the wildlife cops on speed dial," he added with a low hoot.

"Not everybody has the wildlife cops on speed dial," I told him. "IN fact, I'd guess almost no one has the wildlife cops on speed dial."

"What's he talking about?" Wyatt asked.

"He does look like a horned owl," I said, turning to the werewolf. "And that means it's illegal to keep him as a pet. If we get caught with him, he could get confiscated."

Lothian's brow furrowed in confusion. "But you always keep him on a perch in the store," he pointed out.

Ami tapped her finger against the rough wooden table, her eyes fixed on us. "We're witches," she said, her voice laced with confidence. "And the people who come into our store know that. None of them would turn us in."

She gestured to the open doors and windows that overlooked the backyard to emphasize her point. "We have a lot of magical wards and charms on the house and the store," she continued. "So we're protected from a lot of these things."

"But we still need to be careful," I cautioned, my voice low. "We don't want to take any unnecessary risks."

Emma turned to Wyatt, her expression curious. "Hey, do we have those things?" she asked.

Wyatt furrowed his brow, looking puzzled. "What kinds of things?" he asked, his tone uncertain.

"Wards. Charms. Protection spells," Emma clarified.

Wyatt's expression shifted from curiosity to seriousness, and he turned to meet Lothian's gaze. His icy blue eyes searched for answers, and his frown conveyed a sense of internal debate over what course of action to take.

"We have some basic protections in place," Lothian said, breaking the silence.

"Cool." Emma nodded. "Like?"

Lothian and Wyatt exchanged a meaningful glance, their expressions solemn. It was clear that they had more to say, but they were hesitant to speak for some reason.

The room fell silent as we all waited, the tension growing with each passing moment. Finally, Lothian cleared his throat and spoke up.

"We're protected."

"Right, but how?" Emma asked him.

The werewolves in the room shifted, their unease palpable.

Lothian spoke up, his voice low but firm. "We have numerous natural defenses," he said. "Trust us, Hunter is quite safe there."

Wyatt nodded in agreement, his jaw set in determination. "As are you," he added. "You're both very safe. Well-protected."

Emma's eyes darted back and forth between Lothian and Wyatt, her expression a mix of amusement and frustration. "Yes, cool," she said. "I got that. But how do we actually do that?"

Lothian and Wyatt exchanged a knowing glance, their expressions grim.

Archie let out a gasp, his eyes wide with amusement. "Wow," he said. "I'm practically basking in the light of trust here."

Lothian and Wyatt did not look amused at all.

The owl fluttered down to the table, snatched a garlic knot, and then flew back to his perch. "I guess it's less of an alliance between us and more like a semi-lubricated cooperative with occasional diplomatic relations," he mused. "And bacon."

CHAPTER TEN

"What do you mean, Archie?" Ami spun around to face me when he didn't answer, her expression curious. "What does he mean?" she asked, her eyes fixed on mine.

I glanced at the two men on the other side of the table. Lothian pulled at his collar and shifted in his seat while Wyatt's eyes darted around, his hands making minor adjustments to his clothing.

Wow.

So Archie was right.

I cleared my throat, breaking the tense silence in the room. "Archie means that Wyatt and Lothian don't want to reveal what protections they have on their wolf den in front of a bunch of witches," I explained.

Ayla furrowed her brows in confusion. "Is it a pack thing?" she asked. "Like some oath they take not to talk about it or something?"

The two men remained silent, their eyes meeting in an understanding. It was clear that they were hesitant to reveal any more information.

"I don't think so, dear," Aunt Gwennie said, placing a hand on Ayla's arm.

The tension in the room was palpable. I could see the hurt and anger in the eyes of my companions as they grappled with the revelation that these men were keeping secrets from us.

Ami spoke up, her voice hurt. "Why can't you tell us?" she asked. "Don't you trust us? We let you into our house and don't hide anything from you. Our place isn't warded to keep you out."

Lothian broke the silence. "Look, it's not that we don't trust you or that we can't tell you," he said, his voice calm and even. "It's that—"

"Oh, please," I said. "You don't trust us."

Lothian spoke up, his voice calm and even. "Look, it's not that we don't trust you or can't tell you," he said. "We are responsible for protecting our pack, which means being careful about what we reveal. To anyone."

"Enough with the tap dance answers already,"

Archie said, his eyes flashing with annoyance. "If you're not going to tell us what's going on, at least have the decency to say so instead of trying to dance around the issue."

"I did say so," Lothian told him. "I'm not going to tell you."

There was a moment of awkward silence as we all looked at one another, unsure of what to say or do next.

A sharp bark cut through the air before anyone could say anything else.

* * *

THE TINY PUPPY was a bundle of energy, with black and brown fur that shone in the dim light of the room. Its long legs pumped rapidly as it ran up the back porch stairs and into the house through the open French doors, its tail wagging excitedly behind it. Its bright amber eyes sparkled with excitement, almost glowing in the room's dim light, and its perked-up ears seemed to be listening for any sound or movement.

"Is that a puppy?" Ayla asked.

Emma was taken aback as the small, fluffy creature bounded into the room, its tongue lolling out of its mouth and its tail wagging furiously. Its furry legs carried it across the room in no time, and before Emma knew it, it had scampered under her chair.

"It is." As she leaned down to take a closer look, the puppy looked up at her with big, bright eyes, its little tail still wagging excitedly. Emma couldn't resist the puppy's playful energy and scooped it up into her arms, feeling its soft fur against her skin.

"It's a little boy puppy, isn't it?" she cooed. "He's such a cute boy. Yes, he is." The puppy snuggled into Emma's lap, its small body wriggling with delight as she stroked its head and scratched behind its ears. "Where did you come from? Are you lost?"

Glancing over at Lothian and Wyatt, I noticed their faces had gone pale, their eyes wide with barely contained horror.

Wyatt was transfixed by the sight of the puppy, which was now struggling to break Emma's grasp so it could launch onto the dining table. His lips were parted in a silent scream, and his eyes were locked onto the tiny creature as though he had seen a ghost.

Meanwhile, Lothian looked like he might have been on the verge of losing the dinner he had just eaten, his face contorted in disgust and fear.

"Are you going to tell them?" Archie asked Lily, his eyes flickering over to the two werewolves.

The crow shook her head. "I don't think the creature that brings the truth to this table tonight will be thanked for it. I'll remain silent."

Archie nodded in agreement. "For once, I agree with you."

Althea looked at Lily, her eyes narrowing in suspicion. But she turned back to the table and said nothing, seemingly content to let the matter drop.

Meanwhile, Cerberus was jumping around Emma, barking excitedly at the sight of the little puppy in her arms. The small dog squirmed and wriggled, eager to play with the larger dog. Cerberus playfully batted at Emma's hand, trying to free the puppy from her grasp so the two could play together.

Watching the two dogs play, I couldn't help but think about how difficult it was to distinguish between dog breeds when they were still puppies. Greyhound puppies, for example, looked nothing like their sleek, barrel-chested adult counterparts, while a Saluki pup could easily be mistaken for a lab to the untrained eye. And when it came to dog identification, my eye was definitely untrained.

But when it came to identifying paranormals, even as babies?

I was well-versed. It was a skill that had been honed over years of training and experience and was essential to my previous work in the military as I crept in and out of the shadowy world of the supernatural.

The puppy's thick muscles bulged under his fluffy fur coat, and his ears were almost perfect triangles, giving him a fierce and regal appearance. But the length of his muzzle gave away his breed, lending him an air of grave seriousness that was typical of his species.

"Where did you come from?" Emma asked.

The puppy barked.

I sighed.

It looked like I would be the one to tell Emma. I was a little surprised she hadn't clued in yet. The puppy zeroed in on her immediately, his eyes bright with excitement as he looked up at her with a mixture of curiosity and affection.

"He doesn't have a collar," Emma said as she deftly handled the wiggling pup.

"He doesn't need one," I told her, a half-smile on my face. "It would cause a problem for him when he shifts back."

Emma looked at me, her eyes wide with

disbelief. "When he shifts back," she said in a voice laden with dread and horror, her hands shaking as the puppy licked her face. "No. This isn't…it can't be."

Just when Emma thought things couldn't get any worse, Rex (Emma's brother and a vampire) burst through the French doors with a wild look of panic. His eyes darted around the room, searching for something, and his movements were tense and erratic.

"Is Hunter here?" Rex demanded, his voice strained with worry. "Is he all right?"

Emma looked anxious in the face of her brother's frantic state. She tightened her grip on the little puppy nestled in her lap as if trying to steady her nerves.

Rex's eyes finally landed on the furry bundle in Emma's arms, and he sighed in relief even though vampires didn't actually breathe. "Thank goodness," he muttered. "When I woke up, I caught his scent in the wind and could tell he was alone. I was worried he'd gotten lost or hurt."

My gaze flicked toward Lothian and Wyatt, and they both seemed frozen in place. Lothian's eyes were wide and unblinking, and his mouth hung slightly open. Wyatt, meanwhile, had gone completely still, as if he was holding his breath.

Emma set Hunter down gently on the floor, her movements slow and deliberate. She crouched beside him and fixed her gaze on the little puppy, her expression stern.

"You stay right here, young man," she said, pointing her index finger in the air for emphasis. "Do you understand me?"

I couldn't help but smile at the sight of Emma trying to discipline a tiny ball of excited fur. But there was also something heartwarming about the way she cared for Hunter—it was clear that he meant the world to her.

As Emma straightened up and turned to face us, I noticed a flicker of uncertainty in her eyes. "Can Hunter understand me when he's like that?" she asked, gesturing toward the puppy, now sniffing curiously at the hem of her pants.

Wyatt and Lothian exchanged a quick glance, their faces tense with uncertainty. I could tell they were struggling to find the right words to say. Wyatt's gaze dropped to the floor, and Lothian cleared his throat before speaking.

"That's an excellent question," he said, his voice tinged with hesitation. "I can't really tell unless I shift."

"Then do it. Now," Emma ordered, her tone firm and unwavering.

Lothian nodded in agreement, but his expression was pensive as he shifted his weight from one foot to another. I could sense his reluctance, but after a moment of hesitation, Lothian closed his eyes and took a deep breath.

When his eyes opened again, they were glowing an eerie yellow. As his limbs and body stretched, his skin began to ripple and contort, and his clothing began to tear. In the blink of an eye, it seemed like his entire body was encased in fur, and a muzzle appeared from his previously human face. Sharp, pointed canines protruded from his lips as his bones realigned and his body transformed into a full-fledged wolf.

"Wow," Ayla breathed. "That was something."

Lothian let out a low, menacing growl. The sound echoed through the room, drowning out all other noise and announcing his transformation's completion. All that remained of his once-expensive clothes were a few tattered shreds of fabric on the floor.

The room fell silent as we gazed in awe at the magnificent creature before us. It suited him, somehow.

Honestly, he was stunning.

His fur was a black, gray, and white patchwork, and the white shone like moonlight on fresh snow.

The wolf's eyes glowed a menacing yellow, and his sharp, pointed teeth seemed to glint in the soft dining room light. Lothian moved with a graceful, fluid motion despite his size, his large and powerful body slinking like a predator as he scanned the area.

"Okay, that's done with," Emma said, unimpressed, her hand outstretched toward the wolf. "I'm going to ask you again. Can Hunter understand me?"

Lothian sniffed at her hand, his tongue lolling out of his mouth in a canine grin. Despite the menacing aura he exuded, there was a sense of playfulness in his demeanor, a hint of mischief lurking beneath the surface. He seemed to nod once.

"Good," Emma said, her voice firm but gentle. She turned her attention to Hunter, now sniffing at Lothian's paws. "You sit still," she instructed, pointing her finger at the little puppy. "And you stay here. Understand? No running off."

Hunter cocked his head to one side, his tail wagging furiously. He looked up at Emma with his big, innocent eyes as if trying to figure out what she meant.

I couldn't help but chuckle at the sight of Hunter's eager enthusiasm, but I quickly suppressed my amusement when I heard Emma's sharp voice.

"Are you laughing?" she asked me, her tone accusing.

"No," I said, shaking my head. "No, of course not."

Emma raised an eyebrow at my response, clearly unconvinced. "You really need to learn to lie better," she said dryly, a hint of amusement in her voice.

Lothian gave a short bark, and the little puppy immediately stopped his playful prancing and scurried over to sit obediently at Emma's feet. It was clear to everyone in the room that Hunter either ignored or didn't understand Emma's commands, but Lothian's sheer size and dominance had brought the puppy to heel.

"Thank you," Emma said, a note of relief in her voice. "You have my gratitude, Lothian."

Lothian nodded slightly in response to Emma's words, his eyes gleaming with a fierce intelligence. Despite the wolf's intimidating size and power, there was a gentleness in his gaze that spoke of his loyalty and respect for Emma.

Emma pulled out her phone and dialed Eddie's number, a determined look on her face.

She hit the speaker button to ensure we would hear every word he said.

As soon as he answered, she said, "Eddie, it's Emma. I need you to bring the baby to Astra's place right away. I'll explain everything when you get here."

There was a brief pause on the other end of the line, and I could sense the uncertainty in Eddie's voice when he spoke. "Uh, okay. What's going on?"

"I'll explain when you get here," Emma said, her tone urgent. "Just hurry. Time is of the essence."

"On my way," Eddie said before hanging up.

Emma tilted her head back and looked up at Wyatt, her expression stern. "Don't you dare call him back and tell him that Hunter shifted, snuck out of the house, ran across town, and wound up here. Do you understand me?"

Wyatt hesitated for a moment before responding. "I—"

"I'm not asking you," Emma said, cutting him off. "I'm telling you." She turned her gaze to Lothian, her voice taking on a harder edge. "You, either. If either of you gives him the heads up, I will never trust you again."

"Emma—"

"Actually, any of you," Emma continued, interrupting Althea. "Eddie needs to learn that even though he can turn himself into a big dog, it doesn't make him a better parent, mate, or anything."

Her words had a sense of finality that left no room for argument.

I could feel the tension in the air. A feeling of unease that came with knowing that we were in a delicate situation that, frankly, none of us had any business being in.

Aunt Gwennie's eyes narrowed in concern as she watched Emma's determination. "Are you sure you want to do this, Emma? It's a harsh way to teach someone you love a lesson."

Emma took a deep breath, her expression resolute. "Aunt Gwennie, if he calls me and tells me that Hunter's missing, we won't have much of a problem." Her fists clenched at her sides, and she turned to face her brother. "But if he doesn't do that immediately? As soon as he notices Hunter's missing?"

Rex reached out to Emma, pulling her close. There was a sense of tenderness in how he held her, a silent acknowledgment of the bond between them even though she was human and he was a vampire.

With a deep exhale, Emma wrapped her arms around her brother, her cheek pressing against his chest. "Promise me you won't kill him when he gets here."

Rex squeezed Emma in an uncharacteristically tight embrace, his eyes gleaming with a fierce protectiveness. His lips twisted into a slight frown as he muttered, "Well, not right when he gets here."

CHAPTER ELEVEN

Suddenly, the tense silence of the room was shattered by two wolves racing in through the French doors, their sides heaving with exertion. I could sense their movements' urgency and the fierce determination that drove them forward.

As they stopped before us, I couldn't help but feel a sense of awe at their strength and power. With the three of them, it was clear they were magnificent creatures, their fur sleek and glistening in the moonlight, their eyes glowing with fierce intelligence.

They were also in so much trouble.

So much trouble.

For a moment, there was a sense of stillness in

the air, as if everyone in the room was holding their breath, waiting for what would come next. And then, with a sudden burst of movement, the wolves were off again, their powerful bodies streaking across the room toward Emma.

"No! Sit down," Emma commanded with a firmness that left no room for argument. It was as if she were a dog trainer, and the wolves were border collies training for an agility course.

They slowed their walk, but they didn't stop.

And they didn't sit.

"I said sit down!" Emma's voice cracked like a whip, her tone firm and commanding. The wolves hesitated, their eyes locked on Emma's. The beasts slowly lowered their colossal frames to the ground with a heavy thud.

"Well, there's something I never thought I'd see," Archie murmured.

"When you realized Hunter wasn't in his crib," she continued, her voice rising with each word, "did it even once occur to you to pick up a telephone and call me? You know, like a normal father?"

"Emma?"

"What?" she asked me, her frustration and anger palpable.

I knew she was seething inside, her glare

making it hard to meet her gaze. I cleared my throat and spoke softly, almost apologetically. "They can't answer you in that form."

"I know that!" Emma let out a frustrated sigh. "Well, maybe I just want to yell for a while uninterrupted!" she snapped.

I couldn't help but chuckle at Emma's outburst, despite the seriousness of the situation. She had always been a firecracker, but there was something different about her now, a rawness in her voice that spoke of a deep-seated resentment she couldn't quite manage.

Aunt Gwennie arched an eyebrow in disbelief as I tried to stifle my laughter. "You really do laugh at the most inopportune times, Astra," she said.

"She always did find the dark funny," Ami said.

"Sorry! Sorry. I'll be quiet."

For a moment, there was an awkward silence in the room, as if everyone was unsure what to say next. But then Emma's expression softened, and she shook her head.

"No, I'm sorry," she said, her voice almost a whisper. "I know it's kind of funny. I'm not usually like this. But I'm just so frustrated! I don't understand why things have to be so complicated." Hunter lay contently in her arms, his tail wagging slowly as she turned to me. "They're always so wrapped up in their little world of magic, packs, and werewolf stuff that they forget about the real world. He couldn't even call me! It's maddening. How am I supposed to deal with this?"

Emma's eyes glistened with tears as she spoke, her voice trembling with a weariness that came from living in a world full of supernatural beings. Her slumped posture, bowed shoulders, and downturned lips all spoke to the weight of responsibility she felt. I felt a twinge of sadness, not fully understanding her challenges yet wanting to do something to ease her burden.

My mouth opened to respond, but Wyatt beat me to it, his deep voice gentle yet firm. "You're right, Emma," he said. "We're not normal men."

She winced and clutched Hunter tighter. "Wait, I didn't say you're abnormal—"

"No, it's true. We are not like other men. There are differences about us that make us...difficult mates. And I am sorry, truly sorry, that pains you."

I could sense a feeling of openness and honesty in Wyatt's words, a sense that he was willing to acknowledge the challenges that came with being a werewolf in a world of humans.

Althea's gaze softened as she watched him, her dark eyes wide with empathy.

In fact, all my sisters seemed quite taken by Wyatt's little speech.

On the other hand, Rex crossed his arms and glared at the werewolves, his body tense and protective behind his sister. His nostrils flared, and his brow knit as he watched them, radiating a fierce determination.

Whatever empathy the rest of us were feeling? Rex wasn't.

"But that doesn't mean we can't be good men," Wyatt continued. "We can choose to be. We can be the best version of ourselves for those we care about in both forms. I'll admit it is not easy for a werewolf to understand and respect the complexities of human relationships at times, but for those we love, we can learn."

Emma's shoulders slumped, and her gaze drifted to the floor. "I know," she said, her voice quavering with exhaustion. "Well, I don't know. I don't know anything, really. I see that more and more every day."

Wyatt turned to her, his gaze warm and reassuring. "All you need to know is this: we are more than just a group of individuals—we are a family, bonded together by a strength and loyalty that knows no bounds."

As he spoke, his words had a sense of conviction, a feeling of unity and solidarity that was a little infectious. I looked around the room and saw that we all felt the same—a sense of belonging and purpose from being part of something greater than ourselves.

Ami reached out and gently held my hand, her fingers wrapping around mine. I looked at her, squeezed her hand, and smiled.

"As the mother of our youngest pack member," Wyatt continued, "you are part of that now. And no matter what happens, we will always be here for you, ready to support and protect you however we can." He gave the largest wolf a quick glance. "Truly. No matter what happens."

"Thank you," Emma said, her expression one of gratitude. Her mouth curved in a slight smile, but her eyes were uncertain. "I appreciate that. But I need to know right now why my infant son could get all the way across town without any of the werewolves noticing he was gone."

* * *

THE THREE LARGE, muscled men looked positively ridiculous in the flowing priestess robes we had hastily lent them, the fabric draping awkwardly over their broad shoulders and muscular frames. Their wide chests and thick arms strained against the fabric, creating an amusingly ludicrous spectacle.

At least they were now covered and decent, even if they looked absurd.

"I think they look hot," Ayla said. "Very gender-bending."

"You're kidding me. It's not exactly the most dignified outfit," I said with a chuckle, "but it'll have to do. Now," I said, clapping my hands and attempting to take a more serious tone, "let's get to the bottom of this. What exactly happened? I thought werewolves don't shift until puberty?"

Hunter's tail swept back and forth like a metronome as he bounded toward me, his bark joyful and loud. His tongue hung from his mouth, and his eyes shone with excitement.

"Before we get into this, what can he understand?" Emma asked. "I don't want to talk about this in front of him if he should be shielded from this. A two-month-old baby doesn't understand things, but that puppy made it across

Forkbridge, so I'm not taking anything at face value here."

Eddie sat stoically to the right side of Lothian, his muscular frame clad in a deep crimson priestess robe that draped awkwardly over his broad shoulders. He was clearly in pain, both from the trauma of Hunter's disappearance and the weight of his responsibilities as a werewolf and a father.

"In wolf form, he appears to understand slightly more than he would understand in human form, but Astra is right—infants don't shift. I've never heard of a werewolf shifting before they could walk," Lothian told Emma. "Hunter seems to be some kind of werewolf prodigy."

Emma's shoulders sagged, and a groan escaped her lips. Her eyes rolled to the ceiling, and she muttered, "Oh, great. Just what I needed." Emma threw her hands up in the air and sighed. "What do you all know about one another when you're wolves? Can you talk to Hunter? Can he talk to you?"

I was speechless—how did Emma not know this already?

After living with a pack of werewolves and spending time with Eddie, it was almost unbelievable she didn't have this knowledge already. Had she been avoiding confronting the truth?

In the face of my shock and confusion, I could only remain silent.

It wasn't the time.

"We can sense each other's emotions," Wyatt explained. "And we can communicate with one another telepathically while in wolf form. We can also find each other, sense each other's presence."

"That's how Hunter was able to come to find you," Lothian explained. "Even though you're not a wolf, he has that tie to you because you birthed him. He can sense your emotions, he can sense your presence, and he can find you."

Wyatt nodded. "Hunter missed you, and so he came to find you."

As Lothian and Wyatt explained, Eddie and Lawrence (the werewolf Eddie had brought with him) listened intently but added nothing, their expressions giving nothing away. They sat there, still and silent, as their werewolf brothers tried to make sense of the situation for Emma.

Ultimately, it was clear that mere words would not sway Emma.

Her rage flared once more as she spun around to face Eddie, eyes blazing with anger and accusation. "How could you not have heard our son shift into a werewolf and run out of the house?" she demanded. "I thought the whole point of that ridiculous enclave was so you could see people coming and going? How could you not see him going?"

Emma's voice rose with each word, a sharp and cutting edge that sliced through the tense silence of the room. I could feel the rawness of her emotions, the deep well of frustration and disappointment that lay beneath her words.

Eddie, for his part, looked like he had been punched in the gut. He hung his head low as if he couldn't bear to look at her.

"I don't know," he said, his voice low and defeated. "I'd put Hunter down to sleep for the night, and the baby monitor was silent, so I laid on the couch to nap. It's not an excuse, though. I don't know how I missed it." A pause. "I'm sorry."

It was as sincere an apology as I'd ever heard.

And Emma was having none of it.

She leaned forward, her hands clenched into fists at her sides, and glared at him with an almost frightening ferocity.

Hunter whimpered and squirmed.

"Sorry isn't good enough," she said, glaring at Eddie with a look so intense it seemed to burn through him. "Our son was missing, and you had no idea where he was. Do you understand how serious this is? And on top of that, when you realized he was gone, you didn't even bother to call me! You and Lawrence just raced out of the house to look for him!"

Aunt Gwennie pushed her chair back from the table, her lips pursed and her eyes narrowed. "That's it," she said, her voice firm and final. She rose to her feet, her fists clenched at her sides. "I've had enough of this insanity."

* * *

AUNT GWENNIE WASN'T WRONG.

About the insanity, I mean.

It was a surreal scene, one that seemed almost too absurd to be real.

In the large room, there were five witches— my aunt, my three sisters, and myself—gathered around a long wooden table. Beside us were five werewolves, with three of them adorned in long flowing robes that made them look like extras from a Shakespearean play. To round out the group, there was a vampire and a human.

Oh, and let's not forget the three familiars.

Fifteen people gathered together to witness a

couple fight over the care of their child. None of this was our business, and yet in the crazy world we lived in, it kind of was.

It was a scene that would have been comical if it wasn't so serious.

Aunt Gwennie's sudden outburst startled everyone in the room. Surprised, we all looked at her as she marched toward Emma and Eddie with determination in her eyes.

"Goddess bless, Emma Sullivan," Aunt Gwennie said in that warm, southern tone that always hinted at a pending wallop. "I know you're scared and angry, but you need to calm down. This isn't helping anyone." Her eyes flicked to Eddie, who was still sitting silently beside Lothian, and then back to Emma. "You both have to come together for your son's sake. Stop making this about yourselves and start thinking about Hunter. That boy deserves a family who can put aside their differences and work together."

"Excuse me? Who are you to tell me how to manage my family?" Emma bristled at Aunt Gwennie's words, her eyes flashing with fury.

"What family? No matter how often he asks you, you won't marry him, and with all the blame you're casting, it's a wonder he keeps asking!"

Emma's eyes widened. "Aunt Gwennie—"

"I'm the one who had to stay here and pick up the pieces after Astra abandoned this family like her behind was on fire," Aunt Gwennie retorted, her jaw clenched tight. "I've lived here and watched a coven balance on accusations, assumptions, and lies until it killed the High Priestess and an innocent. I know what a toxic family looks like, young woman, and you're getting a bang-up start to yours."

I leaned forward. "I don't really think we need to bring me into this—"

"You peep down, Miss Thing," Aunt Gwennie interrupted me sharply.

I recognized that it was best to defer to her wisdom, so I responded with a "Yes, ma'am" and then peeped down.

Aunt Gwennie's sudden outburst took us all by surprise. Even Emma, who was still seething with anger, was taken aback. Gwennie had always been the calm one in our family, the voice of reason when things got heated. But now, her face was flushed with anger, and her hands were balled up into tight fists.

Emma opened her mouth to respond, but Aunt Gwennie cut her off. "Don't you dare. I'm not done, young lady, and my age and experience means that you all have to sit there and listen to this," she said.

Emma leaned back and nodded.

Turning to Eddie, Aunt Gwennie told him, "You messed up big time. Not because you lost your son but because you raced out of the house to find him partly so you could hide what happened from Emma. She's not an idiot. Relationships with secrets are built on quicksand, young man. You act like you're the only one that's ever been through this, but I have news for you—coven, pack, family? It's all the same."

Eddie turned to Aunt Gwennie and gave a respectful nod.

"And you. I know you're upset, Emma," she said, her voice low. "And you have every right to be. But this is not the way to handle it. Eddie made a mistake, yes. But he's not the enemy here. We need to focus on finding out how Hunter was able to shift so early and what that means for him going forward—and you, little human woman, are not going to figure that out from a book."

"Actually, she might be able to find...it...in...." Althea's voice trailed to a whisper under Aunt Gwennie's withering glare.

"What did I say?" Aunt Gwennie asked. "I know you've all been ignoring your Aunt

Gertrude and me lately, but we've been hovering around here watching over all of you." Aunt Gwennie's eyes narrowed, and the room grew silent, her voice stern and her gaze unwavering. "We know when you've been sleeping and when you're awake. We know all of it. And we're done holding our tongues."

Aunt Gertrude was our aunt.

She's a ghost.

It made her meddling challenging to spot.

"See?" Lily sniffed on Althea's shoulder. "This table does not appreciate the truth."

Aunt Gwennie had always been the right hand of the matriarch of our family. Despite my mother's passing, she didn't try to take on the mantle of the matriarch herself. Instead, she took on a more supportive role, allowing my sisters and me to find our own paths within the family.

But now?

Her patience—and my spectral aunt's—seemed to have reached its limit.

I had never seen her so angry before. It was like a storm cloud had descended upon us, crackling with energy and waiting to unleash its fury. Her eyes blazed with a fierce intensity, and her jaw was set in a hard line as she glared at Eddie.

I stayed silent, knowing better than to argue with her.

"Lily?" Aunt Gwennie asked.

"Yes?"

"Be quiet," she said, her voice like a whipcrack.

The crow tossed her head and looked indignantly at my aunt. However, she remained quiet, probably sensing what would happen if she didn't.

"I've stayed in the background and watched from the shadows, allowing all of you to make whatever mistakes you're going to make so you can learn from them. As it should be." She paused, taking a deep breath before continuing. "But this is where that ends. That is a baby," she said, pointing to Hunter. Then, her gaze moved to Emma. "You chose to mate with a werewolf." She turned to Eddie. "You chose to mate with a human. The two of you had a child with one another. So, stop these petty grievances, and work this out!"

Her words hung in the air, heavy with authority and a sense of finality.

CHAPTER TWELVE

The sudden knock on the door sent a jolt through everyone in the room, causing a few to jump in their seats.

Granted, that was mostly because almost everyone we knew was standing or sitting in the room listening to Aunt Gwennie ream everyone within earshot. It wasn't just Aunt Gwennie's scolding that had everyone on edge. Hunter's early shifting and the tension between Emma and Eddie certainly didn't help our nerves.

Feeling on edge, I asked Ami, "Are you expecting someone?"

Althea chimed in, "Who, me?"

"No, I was talking to—oh, never mind." I pushed off my chair and stood up. "The question could apply to anyone. Is anyone here expecting a visitor?" I checked my phone and saw that it was past nine o'clock. I looked back up. "No one?"

Aunt Gwennie raised an eyebrow, her eyes scanning the room before landing on the door. "Let me see who it is," she said, her tone firm and no-nonsense.

"Don't worry, Aunt Gwennie," I said, a hint of amusement in my voice. "I've got this. You just take a seat and recover from your outburst. Perhaps a glass of water would help. Maybe a bourbon?"

Aunt Gwennie's stern voice cut through the air. "You watch your tone, young lady," she said.

"I will watch my tone, ma'am." I couldn't help but feel slightly amused at Aunt Gwennie's no-nonsense attitude. She may have been old-fashioned in her ways, but she was also a force to be reckoned with. I knew we could always count on her to keep us in line, no matter how chaotic things got.

The witch shop always closed promptly at six o'clock. While we occasionally had the odd customer show up at our doorstep with an incense emergency or a desperate need for a black candle shaped like a male appendage, most of our clientele knew that Arden House was also our residence. They wouldn't dream of disturbing us this late at night.

As I stepped forward to take charge of the situation, I felt a twinge of satisfaction at the opportunity to shift the focus away from Eddie and Emma's romantically entangled parenting disagreements.

While I loved them both dearly, being stuck in the middle of their issues was uncomfortable.

That, and I had no idea how to help them.

I approached the front door and turned the handle. The cool evening air rushed in, bringing the sound of rustling leaves and the distant hum of traffic. As I peered into the darkness, my eyes slowly adjusting to the lack of light, I saw a figure standing just beyond the threshold.

Henry Johnson, holding a tire iron in his hand.

"Henry," I said, my eyebrow arching in surprise as I took in his unexpected arrival. "What brings you here at this hour, holding a weapon I could easily disarm you of?"

Henry looked at me, his expression a mixture of confusion and uncertainty. "Disarm me?" he repeated, his voice rising with disbelief.

"Just want to be clear."

Henry's eyes flickered nervously, his grip on

the tire iron tightening. "Is Emma here?" he asked, his voice tinged with calm and panic.

"She is, but she's…busy." I glanced back into the living room and saw Emma cradling the young wolf in her arms, gently stroking its fur as it nuzzled into her embrace. "What do you need?" I paused, waiting. He looked conflicted. "May I again point out I would be much less on edge during this conversation if you dropped the tire iron?"

Henry's expression was tense as he began to speak, his voice shaking slightly. "I found this tire iron in my backyard," he said, his eyes darting back and forth as if he was afraid someone might be listening in. "And there's blood on the end of it."

Uh oh.

"Blood," I repeated.

He nodded.

"Are you hurt? Did you hit someone or something with it?"

"No, no. It's not mine. My blood. Or my tire iron. I don't know whose it is." He shook his head quickly, his eyes wide as saucers. "I just found it and…I didn't know what to do. I didn't know who else to turn to."

I could sense his fear radiating from every

pore as his knuckles turned white as he tightly clutched the tire iron with one hand and the door frame with the other. He desperately wanted to come inside—but inside was a bunch of witches, a pack of werewolves, and some brilliant (and very illegal) "pets."

"How did you know to come here?" I asked, trying to keep my tone calm and reassuring.

"I went to Emma's house first, and her roommate, Norden, told me she was over here," he said, his grip on the tire iron tightening. His voice trembled with a mixture of fear and uncertainty. "Astra, can I come in?"

I made a mental note to talk with Norden and then hesitated momentarily, considering the potential consequences of letting this human I didn't know into our full-house supernatural safe haven murder meet-up.

With a bloody weapon.

My instinct told me it would probably be okay.

Unless my instinct was wrong, and he really was a murderer.

"Sure, Henry," I said, stepping back. "Come on in."

I strode confidently into the living room, with Henry trailing nervously behind me. Eddie and

Lothian looked up as we entered, their attention immediately drawn to the tire iron clutched tightly in Henry's grip.

"What's going on?" Eddie asked, his voice laced with concern.

I held up a hand, signaling for him to stay calm. "Henry found this in his backyard," I explained, gesturing toward the tire iron. "My bet is it's Barry Fields' murder weapon."

Eddie raised an eyebrow skeptically. "And why, pray tell, is he carrying it around?"

Henry shifted his weight from one foot to the other, a nervous tic that did not go unnoticed by Eddie and Lothian. "I found it in my backyard," he stammered, his voice trembling. "I thought it might have something to do with Barry's murder."

Lothian's expression was stern as he fixed his gaze on Henry. "So you just reached down and picked it up without any gloves?" he asked, his voice laced with disbelief. "Are you daft, man?"

Henry opened his mouth to answer but then paused, confusion etching across his face. "Wait. Are you wearing a toga?" he asked, dumbfounded, his gaze flickering over Eddie and Lothian's flowing gowns.

"We had a bit of a wardrobe malfunction,"

Lothian explained, a hint of amusement in his voice. "But the Ardens were kind enough to loan us some clothes." He gestured toward Eddie and himself and then flexed his bicep. "These robes were the only things that fit our considerable muscles," he continued, a hint of pride in his voice.

Ayla rolled her eyes. "Oh, come on, dude. Turn it down a notch, huh?"

"He can't," Althea told her. "It's impossible. His head would explode."

Henry turned to Emma, but his attention was quickly diverted by the small, furry creature cradled in her arms. He took a step closer, his gaze fixed on the creature. "Is that a wolf puppy?" he asked incredulously, his voice rising with disbelief.

"Henry, why don't you sit down," I suggested.

"Is she holding a wolf puppy?"

"Okay, let's get it all out of the way. They're in girls' clothes, Emma's holding a wolf puppy, and you're holding a murder weapon—anything else we need to go over? You want introductions?" I asked and proceeded to introduce everyone by name. Some smiled and nodded in acknowledgment, while others stared back at Henry with stony silence.

I'll let you guess who did what.

* * *

EDDIE TURNED TO HENRY, his expression one of concern as he gestured toward the object in Henry's hand. "Let's back up for a moment," he said, his tone serious. "Lothian's right. Why would you pick up a murder weapon with your bare hands?"

Henry looked down at the tire iron, his grip tightening reflexively. "I didn't think about it then," he admitted. "I just saw it lying there and thought it might be important."

"Or you did it," Emma said, her eyes fixed on Henry with a cold, suspicious glare.

His voice rose in panic as he held out the tire iron with both hands. "I didn't do it! I swear!" he exclaimed, his eyes wide with fear. "Check it for prints. You'll see I didn't touch it on the opposite end of the blood! I couldn't have done it."

Eddie stepped forward, his eyes fixed on the tire iron as he reached out to take it from Henry's trembling hands.

"Stop," I said firmly, stepping forward to intervene. "The fewer people that handle that thing, the better. Let me have it." I reached out toward Henry, my fingers outstretched. "I might be able to tell who dropped it on your property."

Henry's incredulous stare met mine, his tone laced with disbelief. "All those stories in the paper about your psychic hand thing aren't true, are they?" he asked, his words a mix of confusion and skepticism.

"Do you want help or a lesson in psychic abilities?" I asked.

Henry handed me the tire iron, and I took it from him carefully, grasping it in the center. As soon as my fingers closed around it, I felt a jolt of electricity shoot through my body, the sensation rippling through me like a shockwave. Images of the strawberry field at night flashed in my mind, and I was transported to a different time and place.

In the darkness, I saw a man in a long cloak and hood, his face shrouded by the black fabric and shadows. He held the tire iron in his hand, its weight heavy and ominous.

As the figure walked menacingly toward Barry between the rows of strawberries, the old man pleaded with him, his voice thick with desperation. "She's my daughter!" Barry cried out, his hands up. "I'm sorry, but I can't take this farm from my daughter! Even if she is a woman. She loves this place! Ex feminis viri, ex viris omnia! I know and believe, but it came from me and belongs to her! I still believe it! I haven't broken any rules!"

As quickly as the vision had appeared, it flickered and disappeared, leaving me back in the present with the weight of the murder weapon heavy in my hand.

"You saw something. I can tell by the look on your face. What did you see?" Henry asked, his voice trembling with anticipation.

I ignored his question and asked him one of my own. "Ex feminis viri, ex viris omnia—what does that mean?"

Henry's eyes widened with surprise at the phrase that echoed in my mind. "It means 'out of women, men are everything,'" he explained, his voice tinged with sadness.

"I've got 'from women to men, from men everything,' according to the translator," Althea said, holding up her phone. "It does sound as misogynistic as what he said, though. Similar sentiment. Where did you hear that?"

I took a deep breath, trying to steady my nerves as I recounted what I had seen. "I saw a man in a cloak and hood holding the tire iron," I said. "He was walking toward Barry in the strawberry field, and Barry was pleading with him as he backed away." I paused, remembering what the man had said about the Latin phrase. "He said something about agreeing with 'ex feminis viri, ex viris omnia' and that he hadn't broken any rules."

Henry's face twisted in disgust as he listened to my explanation. "And you think that the man who killed Barry used that phrase to justify his actions?" he asked, his voice laced with disbelief.

I shook my head firmly, my mind racing with possibilities. "No, the killer didn't say it. Barry said it as the killer—presumably—was coming after him," I explained. "We need to find out what this phrase means and who that man is." I rubbed my forehead, feeling the weight of the investigation bearing down on me. "One thing's for sure. Scarlett didn't kill her father."

"You don't say," Ami said, her eyes fixed on me.

I couldn't help but let out an exasperated sigh at my sister's comment. "I glanced down at the hand holding the tire iron. His nails were dirty, his knuckles rough and calloused. It was definitely a man's hand."

* * *

"SO WE'RE LOOKING for a man in a cloak and hood, who apparently subscribes to some misogynistic bullpucky," Emma said, her eyes scanning the faces of everyone in the room. "Anyone have any leads off the top of their heads?"

There was a collective shake of heads.

"I would have thought you werewolves would be familiar with men that subscribe to misogynistic—" she began, only to be cut off by Aunt Gwennie's sharp reprimand.

"Emma!" Aunt Gwennie's sharp voice cut through the air, her eyes narrowing as she fixed her gaze on Emma. Despite our best efforts to keep a low profile and avoid mentioning any of the obvious supernatural identities in the room that were not public knowledge, it seemed like Emma had let her guard down.

"What?" Emma asked my aunt, her tone defensive.

Oh, dear goddess.

Without waiting to see what other pearls of wisdom would fly out of my best friend's mouth, I stepped forward, my voice firm as I began to lay out a plan of action for our investigation.

"All right, we need to split the work up," I said, my voice firm and in assumptive command. "Ayla and Ami, I need you to start researching that Latin phrase and see if it leads anywhere. Start with gangs or movements that use that phrase. Althea, you take the tire iron to your workshop"—the potion room—"and see if you can find any fingerprints or other evidence on it. But don't get your fingerprints on there, and don't disturb any evidence—non-destructive... um, investigative techniques only. At some point, we'll have to turn it over to the police." I looked at Henry. "Do you have security at your house? Cameras?"

The farmer nodded, his face grim. "Yes, I do. Just basic surveillance cameras. But they're not very good. If you have a computer, I can pull up the footage."

"Lothian, Wyatt, use my laptop with Henry and examine the footage," I said, gesturing toward the device on the table. "See if you can identify anyone who came onto Henry's property and dropped that tire iron."

"Excuse me." Emma stared at me. "Who died and made you the detective in charge?" she asked, her voice sharp with anger.

Hunter's eyes locked onto mine, and he let out a low, rumbling growl.

"Oh, goodness, you're just adorable," I said, my

voice filled with affection as I reached down to stroke the puppy's soft fur. "We need to find out what happened," I told Emma once I pulled my hand far enough back that I felt I could risk talking again. "And if that means taking charge and making tough decisions because you're not able to get your head in the game right now, so be it."

It was harsh. I knew it was harsh.

But it was also true.

I could almost feel the angry heat radiating off her, as if she was a coiled spring ready to explode. She handed Hunter to Rex and clenched her fists so tightly that her knuckles had turned white.

"Emma, come on," I said. "Take it down a notch. You've done this for me."

I couldn't help but feel a sense of guilt and remorse for my words. I knew what I was saying was true, and we needed to stay focused and committed to solving the case she put us on, no matter what. But another part of me recognized the pain and frustration in Emma's eyes, the sense of hurt and betrayal she was undoubtedly feeling.

We all have moments when things seem overwhelming.

This was hers.

Rex moved closer to his sister, his eyes fixed on her as he looked her up and down with a critical eye. "I would have thought those baby hormones would have settled down by now," he said, his voice heavy with weariness. "It must feel like you're on a crazy roller coaster with no end."

The room fell into a heavy silence as soon as Rex finished speaking. Everyone turned to stare at him, taken aback by his callousness.

"What?" Rex asked, his tone incredulous as he noticed everyone's eyes on him. "I'm a vampire. I can sense what's in everyone's blood," he explained, his voice laced with a hint of superiority. "You people really like getting wound up, don't you?"

I bit my lip, trying not to laugh at Rex's comment.

Henry furrowed his brow and leaned in. "Say again? Sorry, I think I misheard you," he said, his eyes widening with confusion. He cocked his head to one side, waiting intently for Rex to reiterate what he just said.

"He's an umpire," Ami told Henry.

Henry nodded slowly in response as if what Ami said made sense.

Emma stepped forward, her eyes blazing with

fury. "You know what, I don't need this. I'm out of here," she spat, storming out of the room…

…and up the stairs to the second floor.

And then the third.

I heard the door to my room slam.

Well, at least she didn't leave.

As much as Emma's attitude grated on me, I knew she was going through an incredibly tough time. Perhaps the most challenging time of her life. As a single mother, she already had her plate full with the daily challenges of raising a child and navigating a complicated romantic relationship. But now, with the added burden of supernatural drama that she didn't understand, her stress and anxiety levels were undoubtedly off the charts.

"I wish I knew what to do for her," Rex told me.

Little Hunter's distress grew. The little pup whimpered and struggled, his eyes fixed on the empty space where his mother had stood. I could feel his pain and confusion like a palpable energy pulsing through the room.

Just as I was about to step forward to try and comfort him, Eddie rushed over to Rex and took the small wolf into his muscled arms. He cradled Hunter gently, whispering words of comfort in his ear. I watched Hunter slowly calm down, his body relaxing in Eddie's embrace.

Despite his rough and tough exterior, Eddie had a heart full of compassion and kindness.

I had no idea why Emma seemed incapable of seeing that.

"I wish I knew what to do for her, too," I told the vampire.

I didn't have all the answers. Heck, I didn't have any answers. Just a determination to do everything in my power to help her through this difficult time.

Right after I figured out who murdered Barry Fields and was framing—

I frowned.

Hold up.

If someone had been determined to frame Henry for Barry's murder, why had Scarlett been the one to end up in a cell?

CHAPTER THIRTEEN

My mind raced with questions and theories as I ascended the stairs to my room, each more complicated and perplexing than the last. Someone had gone to great lengths to frame Henry for Barry's murder, but why? And why had Scarlett been arrested, and where had the overwhelming evidence against her come from?

It didn't make sense, and I couldn't get away from the feeling that something more was going on, something deeper and more sinister than we had previously suspected. I needed more answers and information to put the puzzle together and figure out what was happening.

I needed my best friend.

As I climbed the stairs, I heard a sob from my room. I knocked on the door, taking a deep breath to brace myself.

"Emma? It's Astra. Can I come in?"

There was a brief pause before hearing her muffled voice from the other side. "Yes, it's fine," she said, her voice breaking with emotion. "Come in. It's your room, after all."

I stepped through the door and shut it behind me before climbing the stairs to my attic bedroom.

Emma sat on my bed with her back to me, her gaze fixed on the mirror. It looked like she'd sprayed it with the glowing blue underworld portal concoction Althea'd cooked up so we could talk to Jason and my mother. As I approached, I could see Jason's reflection glowing from within, his face concerned.

I reached out to gently tuck a strand of hair behind her ear as I sat down beside her, but she flinched away, wiping angrily at her tears with one hand.

"It'll be fine, Emma," I assured her softly. "Whatever it is, it will be fine."

"Hey, Astra," my ex-boyfriend, Jason, said from the glowing mirror.

Even though it was only a reflection, seeing Jason's face hit me square in the gut. It brought back so many good and bad memories, and the ache of loss was palpable in my chest.

"Hey, Jason," I said, trying to steady my voice. "What's going on?"

"Emma and I were just talking about what she's been going through since moving into the Werewolf Den," Jason said. "While I never lived at Arden House, I can sympathize with her situation —though ours was far less serious because we didn't have children."

Emma snorted and rolled her eyes. "No, you died as a result of Astra's mother. Not at all serious. Jason is attempting to reassure me that I can adjust to all of the supernatural crap in my life and make my relationship with Eddie work— although you two never did, and being close to you killed him." She gave me a look. "He's not very convincing."

As I heard her words, I winced, feeling the sting.

But I remained silent.

Emma had been through a lot recently, what with her baby-daddy drama and the stress of living in a new, strange place. I could see why she was upset, but it didn't make it any easier to deal with.

"I apologize, Astra. I'm not sure what's wrong with me. I'm not sure how much longer I can stand it," Emma said, her voice quivering with emotion. "Every day feels like a struggle just to keep my head above water."

It was difficult to watch her pain.

I turned to face Jason, his reflection in the glowing mirror flickering. He looked just as I remembered him, dressed in a crisp pair of slacks and a short-sleeved shirt accentuating his lean frame. Even though he lived in the underworld—where the sun could never reach him—his brown hair still had the sun-bleached highlights I had always found so appealing.

"Jason and I didn't work out because I never fully let him into my world, Emma," I explained, shifting my attention from Jason to Emma. "He wanted to be a part of it, but I was too scared to let him in. I didn't want to have to explain my world to him, and I didn't want to guide a human through all the things that came naturally to me. Most importantly, I didn't want to deal with the guilt I'd feel if something bad happened to him." I cast a glance at him. "Doesn't that seem ironic?"

Jason gave a sad smile. "It does, indeed. But, Emma, I believe the lesson here is that what will happen will happen. You can't avoid disaster by shoving people away and keeping them at arm's length." He paused, his face thoughtful. "You have the polar opposite issue that I did. Eddie has opened his life to you so that you now have a pack of werewolves defying their alpha because he told them to listen to you first. That's how much he believes in you. That's how badly he wants you to be a part of him and his life."

Emma sniffed and wiped her eyes once more. "I guess I never thought of it that way."

"He's right, Emma," I agreed with my ghostly ex-boyfriend.

"You must remember that you are still the same person you were before you moved into the Werewolf Den, the same person you were before Hunter. That which makes you, you, at your very essence? That is still the case. You still have the same courage and strength that brought you here. You'll be able to make it work. All you have to do is believe in yourself." Jason gave a wistful sigh. "You don't have to go it alone. Your family, friends, and allies are ready to assist and guide you through these new experiences."

"Thank you, Jason. I really value your advice." Emma nodded, her face still pained but less intense than before.

"Of course, Em. You know I'm always here for you," he said. He gave me a quick glance before turning away. "Astra, take care of yourself."

I swallowed. "You as well," I called after him.

With that, Jason's image faded away from the mirror, leaving us alone in the room.

* * *

"THAT," she explained.

"What?"

"That," Emma said, her voice barely above a whisper, "the way your face twisted with pain and anger for a second as he vanished. It's rather dramatic. It terrifies me. It's as though supernatural things are destined for sadness."

"That is not true. First and probably most important, it's not that dramatic, and it's not supernatural, Emma," I explained. "It's my Greek tragedy, all mine. Neither yours nor anyone else's. All my mother's desire for control and authority drove her Machiavellian schemes—none of which were magical, paranormal, or curse-like. My mother was just a bad person, whether a witch, werewolf, or human. My life will not be yours, and it will certainly not be your son's."

Emma's face softened, and she leaned in closer, the faint scent of baby lotion enveloping me like a warm embrace. "I'm sorry," she apologized softly. "I know I've been a total jerk lately."

I smiled, a ray of hope flickering within me. "You've been through a lot of changes."

"Right. That's a good point."

"Look, I understand how difficult this is for you, and I'm sure your bad-mannered brother was completely right. You're still adjusting to your body's hormone fluctuations. You have a lot on your plate, Emma, but you're strong," I said, resting my hand on her shoulder. "You've already been through so much and have come through it all. You can do it."

Emma let out a long sigh, and I could see the tension in her face diminish. "Thank you," she said with a small smile. "I'm not sure what I'd do without you."

I rolled my eyes, but I really felt warm affection. Emma was like a sister to me, and I loved her, even if she could be a pain in the butt sometimes. "You're welcome," I said, letting my hand fall from her shoulder.

"You know," Emma said. "I've been thinking."

"Oh boy," I said, a smirk playing at the corners of my mouth. "That's always dangerous."

"Shut up," she said absentmindedly. "I was thinking about Scarlett and Henry. Why would a bloodied tire iron be on Henry's property if Scarlett's been arrested for Mr. Fields' murder? What evidence could they possibly have against her if the murder weapon hadn't been found by the police yet?"

"It occurred to me right before I came here, too," I said. "There are a few possibilities. It might not be to frame Henry—it could be a clue planted by the killer to frame Scarlett for the murder. We don't know whose fingerprints are on the tire iron. What if they're hers? Maybe the killer wanted the murder to be linked to Henry. Or wanted Scarlett linked to Henry."

Emma nodded, her eyes narrowing in concentration. "We need to find out whose fingerprints are on the tire iron," she said. "Maybe we'll get lucky, and the killer will have left fingerprints on there."

"I wouldn't get your hopes up, but sure, it could happen," I agreed. "Althea has it now and is working on processing the prints. Hopefully, we won't have to wait too long for the results."

"I'm sorry again for biting your head off." Emma nodded and then stood up, offering me one last hug before she headed back downstairs. "Let's go check on the baby, shall we? Then we can see what Althea has found out about the tire iron and make a plan from there."

I smiled as I hugged Emma back, glad she was beginning to retake an interest in our investigation. "Just don't forget Henry doesn't know about the variety of supernatural beings we have downstairs," I cautioned. "Being part of this team means keeping our secrets safe."

"Right."

We descended the attic staircase one after another, my leading. I glanced back at Emma and wondered if her conversation with Jason had provided enough clarity to tackle this investigation without getting distracted by what was happening in her personal life.

Only one way to find out, I thought.

I glanced back again to ensure she was okay and saw a newfound determination in her eyes. I was relieved—if anyone could solve this case, it was her; Emma Sullivan was one of the best detectives around.

* * *

As soon as we entered the living room, Althea's gaze was drawn away from her computer toward us, a determined expression on her face.

"I've got news!" she said. "The prints on the tire iron belong to three people: Scarlett, Henry, and an unknown third party. Well, four if we count yours—at least when I examined them." She winked. "I'm still trying to figure out who that third person is. I'll keep hacking—um, looking." She blinked innocently and lowered her gaze to her laptop.

"That's great, Althea," Emma said, her voice low and measured. "Any idea about this third person at all? Like, do we know who he's not?"

"Who he's not?" Ami asked.

"You know, not military, not law enforcement," Emma explained. "Who he's not helps us narrow down who he could be."

"No, not even that yet," Althea said, her fingers flitting across the keyboard of her laptop. "I'm searching through many databases and cross-referencing the prints with any criminal or military records, but it's all still running. Don't worry, I'll track them down."

"Any other updates?" I asked.

Lothian nodded from his seat in the corner of the room. "The surveillance footage from Henry's farm wasn't great quality, but I could make out someone that looked like a deputy entering and exiting the property. Their car—unmarked—parked right where Henry said he found the tire iron. It looked like they were there for more than just a routine visit–though we can't be sure what they were doing. The camera coverage isn't great."

"Can't tell if it's a man or a woman?"

Eddie shook his head. "We are wondering why they would go there at such an odd hour. Could they have been planting evidence?" Eddie asked without expecting an answer. "Sure. It's possible. Anything is possible."

"What hour?" Emma asked.

"Nine at night."

"They showed up after Scarlett was already in jail, too," Lothian added.

Emma frowned. "That doesn't make any sense. I mean, if they planted it."

"Wait—you really think a county deputy planted it?" Eddie asked leaning forward quickly. He looked down at Hunter as the slumbering pup suddenly opened his eyes and yelped in worry before slowly lowering his head to his father's feet and dozing off once more. Eddie whispered, "Sorry. You think a deputy planted the murder weapon?"

"Normally, I wouldn't, but you didn't meet Abernathy," Emma told Eddie. "There's something wrong with that guy. I don't know what, but I'm sure it's something." Her lips parted, and she inhaled deeply. "Anyway, putting that jerk aside? It still makes no sense."

My eyes widened as I focused on Henry. "No, it doesn't," I said and moved closer to him, scanning his face for cues. His brow furrowed, unable to meet my gaze. "Do you know why the deputy was on your property, Henry?"

Henry's gaze evaded mine, his posture tense and defensive. He moved his hand with a jerky, spasmodic motion, his trembling fingers betraying the apprehension he felt. "I'm sure there's a reasonable explanation, but I'm not sure what it is."

I scanned Henry's mannerisms, watching him tense and relax as he shifted in his chair. His gaze darted around the room, never settling on any spot for too long. Why was he so jumpy—what was he trying to hide?

This was the second time today that I thought similarly about this guy.

I leaned forward, my brows furrowed as I examined Henry's face. "Forgive me for saying so," I said, "but that doesn't sound very convincing. You have nothing to hide if you're innocent—yet your eyes flicker away when I ask certain questions, and you sometimes hesitate before you respond. Your hand's shaking a little. It's like you're holding back, or maybe even, I don't know—afraid to tell us something?"

Archie sat atop his living room perch, his feathers ruffled as his head turned toward Henry. His enormous yellow eyes were wide and alert. Next to him, Lily, the crow, shifted her wings slowly as she kept her gaze on Henry.

It must be killing those two to keep their beaks shut.

"Astra, the guy did just find a possible murder weapon on his farm," Ami said as she pulled out her well-worn tarot cards. "That would make anyone a little jumpy." She ran her fingers over their edges before revealing several card faces quickly. Her blue eyes locked onto Henry's, studying him. "Though my sister is right. You're hiding something. Something big"

Henry furrowed his brow, rubbed the back of his neck, and peered at the cards in front of Ami. He shook his head in disbelief. "You can tell that from a deck of cards?" he said. "Come on."

Emma raised her arm with a sharp upward motion and ambled toward Henry, their eyes locked. "Why did you come looking for me instead of going to the Forkbridge Police or the sheriff's department?" she asked. "We just met today. You don't know any of us, and yet you brought that thing here instead of where you should have brought it—to the authorities. Why?"

Henry shifted uncomfortably in his seat, his eyes flickering around the room as if searching for an escape. "I – I didn't trust the authorities," he admitted, his voice low and hesitant.

"Why not?" Emma asked.

Henry paused, his eyes slowly lifting to meet hers. His chest remained oddly still as he inhaled a deep breath before speaking. "Because Abernathy's running the investigation, and that guy was sniffing around Scarlett long before any of this happened," he said. "The man's a corrupt son of a—" Henry looked at Aunt Gwennie and stopped himself. "Pardon me, ma'am. He's corrupt. He's got half the police force in Forkbridge under his thumb."

"What do you mean? Sniffing around Scarlett, how?" I asked.

Henry stared into the distance with a weary sigh, his knuckles white as he pressed them against his forehead. "Look, Abernathy's always had it in for witches," he said, pausing for a moment before continuing. "He doesn't trust them—and that includes Scarlett. He asked her about witchcraft and where her coven was meeting—like she had a coven—or like witchcraft was real." His eyes darted to us, apologetic. "No offense," he added.

"None taken," I assured him.

"The guy doesn't seem to think it's just people practicing an old nature religion. He thinks all these myths from history are real. Can you believe that?" Henry's shoulders slumped, and he exhaled a deep sigh.

I could believe that.

"Anyway, the guy's nuts, and his harassment made her really uncomfortable. I figured it wouldn't hurt to come here and ask you lot for help before going to the police because you, Emma, are friends with people that pretend to be witches, too." He looked at me. "Um, no offense—"

"Just get on with the story, Henry, and quit apologizing."

"There's no way Scarlett killed her father, and—"

"How do you know for sure?" I asked.

Emma crossed her arms and tilted her head to the side. "And why do you care?" she added, her voice dripping with intrigue. "Do you usually get this involved with business partners when they run into issues like this?"

Henry's brows drew together, and his eyes seemed to sag in their sockets. He scrubbed his hands over his face in a gesture of evident fatigue and frustration. "I–uh, well, that is..." he stammered, his fingers fidgeting nervously in front of him.

Aunt Gwennie's eyes narrowed, and her lips pressed together in a thin line. "Spit it out, lad!" She gave Henry a long, hard stare. "We don't have all night. I'm an old woman, and it's past bedtime."

Henry took a deep breath and slowly exhaled before finally meeting our gazes. "I'm in love with her," he said, his voice barely audible. He swallowed hard and held up his hands defensively. "It's not what you think—we haven't been together for years, not since high school, but she still means something to me. I can't stand the thought of her being locked away for something she didn't do. She doesn't deserve it."

I groaned, pressing my fingers against my temples.

Fantastic.

Just what we needed: Another chaotic love story.

Clearly, we can't have too many of those.

CHAPTER FOURTEEN

As we descended the stairs, I reached into my pocket, and my fingers brushed against a crumpled paper. "What's that?" I asked myself and remembered the sigil Scarlett had drawn earlier when we visited her at the county jail. I pulled it out, unfolding the creases and smoothing it out as best I could.

"I almost forgot about this," I admitted, holding the paper for Emma to inspect.

Her eyes widened, curiosity mingling with recognition. "Is that the sigil found near Mr. Fields' body?"

"Yeah. We've been so busy running here, there, and everywhere all day I completely forgot I had it."

I handed the paper to Althea, who furrowed her brow in deep concentration. She examined the sigil's deceptively simple design, holding it up to the dim light as if she expected it to reveal a hidden secret. Shadows played across her face as she turned it this way and that, searching for meaning in the cryptic symbol.

Althea's focus lingered for a moment before she sighed and shook her head. "No," she admitted, her voice tinged with disappointment. "I don't think I've ever seen this before. This section somewhat resembles the symbol for male, and that could be a knife, perhaps?" She tilted her head, her eyes narrowing. "Or maybe it's a stick elephant?" She tilted her head the other way, a playful smirk dancing on her lips. "Honestly, I have no idea."

"Are you sure?"

Althea nodded with conviction. "Absolutely. I've encountered countless symbols and glyphs in my time, but this one is unfamiliar."

As Althea's hand extended to return the paper to me, Henry moved, snatching it from her grasp. He held it up to the faint light, his eyes narrowing as he examined the mysterious symbols etched onto the worn page.

A moment later, his eyes widened in

recognition. "Yes," he said, his voice low and thoughtful. "I have seen this before."

Emma and I exchanged a glance, our eyebrows raised in surprise. I noticed Althea leaning in, her curiosity now ignited. "What is it?" she inquired, her gaze locked on Henry as anticipation hung in the air.

"It's like the logo for the Palmetto Society," he said.

"The Palmetto Society?"

Henry nodded. "I got invited to join when I turned thirty-five, but I didn't have the time," he replied. "It's a group of men who have come together to positively impact their towns."

"Like a non-profit?" I asked.

"No. Well, I don't know, really. They're pretty private, so I can't tell you too much about what they do, but it's common knowledge that they have a lot of sway in the community." He pointed to the sigil. "This is on their jackets and hats or something. Anyway, like I said—it's invitation only, and I turned them down, so I don't know much more."

"It sounds like a fraternity," Ayla said.

"For men over thirty-five only?" Althea raised a skeptical eyebrow. "It sounds like a secret society to me, and I've never heard of anything good coming from powerful men forming a secret society."

Wyatt, who had been observing from the sidelines, chimed in. "It's more than your average secret society," he said. "The Palmetto Society has been implicated in some rather unsavory affairs in the past. Nothing concrete, of course— whispers and rumors." His tone carried a note of gravity as he shared his insight.

Emma's eyes widened in surprise, and Althea leaned in closer, her gaze fixed on Wyatt. "What kind of rumors?" the detective asked, her curiosity piqued.

"Yes, do tell," I asked.

It didn't matter which shady stuff it was. Shady was shady.

But my curiosity got the better of me.

Wyatt hesitated as if weighing his words carefully. "There have been whispers of secret meetings in the woods, arcane rituals," he said. "I've heard some accusations of them being involved in illegal activities, too, like money laundering and blackmail."

Emma furrowed her brow, unimpressed. "That's not very specific."

"I haven't come across any detailed allegations," Wyatt admitted.

I turned to Wyatt. "How did you come across all this information? You've only been living here for a few months."

"Let's just say I have my methods," he said, still retaining that enigmatic air. "And I've had my eye on the Palmetto Society for some time."

"Why?"

He shrugged.

"Are they always this annoying?" I asked Emma.

Wyatt and Lothian looked at each other, both of them forcing an expression that could be charitably described as overdone. Wyatt's mouth twitched in a pathetic attempt to appear brokenhearted while Lothian pretended to be deeply aggrieved, his eyes crinkling so much they almost disappeared.

"The melodramatic grandeur twins?" Emma rolled her eyes and nodded. "Yes," she said through gritted teeth. "They're always this annoying."

Each seemed determined to outdo the other in a contest of dramatic despair.

"Enough! Stop it already," I said.

"Well. That hurt," Wyatt said.

He said it with a theatrical pout, too.

"So what's this symbol doing next to Mr.

Fields' body?" I asked. "Why would someone draw the Palmetto Club logo in the dirt at a murder scene? Is the murderer trying to accuse even more people? Muddy the waters?" I couldn't help but let out a sarcastic chuckle. "At this rate, they might as well place an ad in the local paper, listing all their suspects for our consideration."

"Or the Palmetto people might have done it, and one of the members had a guilty conscience," Emma speculated. "Maybe they wanted to make sure Scarlett didn't get blamed."

"That assumes people are trying to frame her," Lothian said.

Ami nodded. "Which we won't know for sure until we can see what evidence the county has collected."

"Which they're never going to show us." Emma's tone held a hint of frustration.

"But they will show Scarlett's attorney," Eddie said. "Do we know who that is?"

"Joe Banning," Henry said. "I talked to him earlier today. I have an appointment with him tomorrow."

"Okay. Then tomorrow, we go see Joe Banning."

* * *

As the sun peeked over the horizon, Emma, Lothian, and I found ourselves outside Joe Banning's office, right on the dot at nine. We'd booked the day's first appointment for ourselves instead of going with Henry, eager to get to the bottom of things (and to keep our distance from Henry publicly for now.) Joe, a lanky figure with a meticulously groomed goatee, appeared as if he'd be more at home navigating the frenetic world of Wall Street than tending to the affairs of our charming little hamlet.

Then again, Scarlett Fields was far from the typical small-town girl embroiled in a murder accusation—and it was becoming apparent that this was no ordinary small-town murder case, either.

"Ah, Astra Arden," Joe said, rising from his desk to shake my hand. "I've heard a lot about you."

I raised an eyebrow. "All good things, I hope."

Joe let out a chuckle. "Naturally. And you must be Emma Sullivan, right?"

"I must be," Emma told him.

We settled into the chairs facing Joe's imposing desk while Lothian remained discreetly behind us. I couldn't help but notice that Joe didn't bother asking about Lothian's identity or role. I wondered if it was a calculated move or a testament to his laser-focused demeanor.

"Now, let's get down to business. What can I do for you two?"

My gaze wandered across the hodgepodge of items strewn about Joe's desk. Piles of legal documents formed miniature towers, accompanied by an assortment of pens and pencils. An ornate wooden box with meticulous carvings piqued my curiosity. However, the sizable paperweight—fashioned into a detailed palmetto leaf—stole my attention. It sparkled center stage amid the chaos.

A thought crossed my mind: could the paperweight be a subtle nod to Joe's affiliation with the Palmetto Society? Or was it a coincidence?

My fingers twitched with the urge to snatch it, yet I struggled to devise a smooth way to do so. The paperweight seemed so close, yet frustratingly beyond my grasp.

"We're here to discuss Scarlett Fields and the murder of Barry Fields," Emma said, her voice calm and measured.

Joe's face morphed into an inscrutable mask, and I sensed the atmosphere in the room tighten. He paused before releasing a heavy sigh. "I can't delve into the specifics, I'm afraid. Attorney-client privilege, you understand."

Emma whipped out her badge, a confident glint in her eyes. "I'm a detective with the Forkbridge Police Department."

Joe's expression remained unchanged, yet I caught a fleeting hint of worry in his gaze. "I appreciate your position, Detective, but unfortunately, I still can't disclose any details about my client's case. I told Henry Johnson the same thing when he came by."

Lothian stepped up, his voice measured. "We don't intend to make you break the law or expose anything that would harm your client's case, Mr. Banning. We're simply curious if you're familiar with the sigil found near the victim's body. We've been attempting to track it down to see if identifying it could help with the investigation, but we've come up short."

Joe's eyes briefly flicked to the paperweight on his desk before locking onto Lothian's stare. "I'm afraid I have no knowledge of that."

Oh, really?

A lawyer should have a better poker face.

Kudos, Lothian.

Joe's voice took on a grave tone. "I can share that I've gone over the county's evidence against

Scarlett. It doesn't paint a pretty picture. The county prosecutor's office has significant evidence stacked against her."

Emma's eyes narrowed. "Why do you say that?"

Joe leaned back in his chair, steepling his fingers together thoughtfully. "Well, for starters, there's the murder weapon. They found it in her house, coated with her fingerprints and the victim's blood. Then there's her motive. Barry Fields altered his will, bequeathing his farm—and a substantial estate—to Brock Taylor. That provides a clear motive. Additionally, witnesses claim to have seen her quarreling with her father on the night of the murder."

"What witnesses?" I asked.

Joe hesitated before continuing. "Off the record, the witnesses have solid reputations. It's unlikely a jury wouldn't find them credible."

Off the record?

We weren't journalists.

My gaze returned to the palmetto paperweight as I schemed to concoct a seemingly innocent way to snatch it up.

"Mr. Banning, is there anything else you can tell us about the case?" Emma asked.

Joe shook his head. "No, I'm afraid not. I can't

say much without risking a conflict of interest. I recommend contacting the county prosecutor's office if you have further questions. They can provide more information than I can from here."

A conflict of interest for lawyers means an attorney's personal interests or obligations clash with their professional responsibilities toward their clients.

Was this guy clueless, or had he just made a Freudian slip?

Emma and Lothian exchanged a glance before she nodded in agreement. "All right, we won't take up more of your time today." We all stood and exited Joe's office, stepping back into the waiting area of the small law firm. "Thank you for seeing us—oh, wow! That painting is fantastic!"

Emma seized Banning's arm and steered him to the far side of the room.

Lothian halted me with a hand on my shoulder, a subtle smirk on his lips. "Did you forget something, Astra? Your purse, perhaps? It must be in the office."

Joe had been so engrossed in our conversation that he hadn't noticed my interest in the paperweight earlier. But I was sure he would know what had happened if I swiped it now.

Should I take the risk?

With a swift nod to Lothian, I slipped back into Joe's office and darted straight for the desk. My heart hammered in my chest as I reached for the paperweight, my fingers curling around its cool, smooth surface. As I lifted it, a jolt of electricity coursed through me, causing me to stumble and drop the paperweight with a resounding clatter.

"You've got to be kidding. You're not warded," I muttered, snatching the paperweight and stuffing it into my pocket. "And you're definitely not warded with electricity. You can't be."

But it was.

On both accounts.

My hip tingled with an electric buzz.

Taking a deep breath, I tried to steady my nerves as I rejoined the others in the waiting area, striving for nonchalance. Emma and Lothian remained immersed in conversation with Joe, but the werewolf's attention snapped to me as I appeared.

"Ready to go?" Lothian asked, a knowing glint in his eyes.

I nodded, struggling to maintain a neutral expression. "Yep, let's get out of here."

Stepping out of the office and into the

brilliant morning sunlight, a wave of relief washed over me. I had the paperweight, and we'd gleaned valuable information about the case, but I couldn't shake the nagging sense that something was amiss.

It wasn't a subtle feeling.

More like a jolt—trying to zap my hip bone with tiny, electric sparks shooting in all directions.

* * *

As we drove away from the lawyer's office, the sun blazed overhead, and I struggled to concentrate on the road despite the intensifying electric current pulsating from the paperweight. When we'd put enough distance between us and the office, I veered onto a quiet, tree-lined side street, parked the car beneath the dappled shade of an old oak tree, and then turned to my companions.

"Listen up," I said, my voice quivering with stress as the paperweight zapped me. "You cannot touch this thing. It's warded, and if someone—someone human—touches that energy, there could be serious consequences." I glanced around, searching their faces for understanding. "I don't know what powers it holds, so please, don't touch it."

Lothian and Emma exchanged an anxious glance before nodding their agreement.

I stepped out of the driver's seat, took the paperweight from my pocket, and held it at arm's length with an oil rag I grabbed from the floor, taking care not to let it touch me as I walked to the back of the Jeep. Retrieving a black box from the trunk with my free hand, I couldn't help but remember that I had "borrowed" it from the magical military upon my departure.

I also couldn't help but remember they still hadn't paid me my pension.

The box, a marvel of enchantment, was lined with magically woven black silk—a fabric designed to sever any mystical connections the item inside might have had with its previous owner or any original spell-caster. With a deep breath, I placed the paperweight in the box and shut the lid.

The tension in my shoulders eased ever so slightly as if the box had managed to contain the paperweight's power and a portion of my anxiety. I returned to the car, climbed back in, and prepared to head out.

"What was it?" Emma asked. "Did you see anything?"

"It was a paperweight," I said. "And it was covered in defensive wards. But not just any wards. They were electricity wards. I felt a jolt of electricity when I touched it. So, no, I haven't read it yet."

Emma's eyes widened in shock. "Electricity wards? That's not something you see every day, I guess. Do you think it's connected to the murder case?"

I shook my head. "I don't know yet. If I had to guess, the lawyer's a member of the Palmetto Society, and the paperweight is given to members of the Palmetto Society, but that's all just speculation." I frowned. "Something's not right with all this, though. That guy believes the county has the murder weapon. But we know we do."

"Yeah, I picked up on that." Lothian leaned forward, his eyes clouding with concern. "Back to the zapper glass—you think it's dangerous?"

"It could be." I shrugged. "I have no idea. But we need to be cautious. I don't want to take any chances with this thing."

"Maybe we shouldn't bring it back to Arden House."

I turned to face him, my eyes locked onto his.

"Where else would we go? Arden House is the most warded and protected place in Central Florida."

Emma nodded in agreement. "She's right. We should take it there, but I'll call Eddie and have him take Hunter back to our house instead of staying at Arden House. Our den. House. Whatever. Whatever. Whatever we call it. Just to be safe."

"Agreed," I said, starting the car and pulling back onto the road.

A nagging unease settled in my stomach as we drove back to Arden House. So many suspects and people claiming to have the murder weapon. It was insane.

I couldn't help but worry that we had stumbled onto something far bigger and more complicated than we'd anticipated.

CHAPTER FIFTEEN

"*I* call and tell you to get the baby out of the house, and you invite your boyfriend over for pancakes?" I asked Ayla, my voice dripping with disbelief as I walked into the house, the air smelling of bacon and lavender. "When I said I was bringing something home that could be dangerous, how did you interpret that statement?"

"To be fair, my pancake flipping skills are legendary," Mel said.

Ayla cocked an eyebrow, winding a lock of her hair around her finger. "You know, Mel's not a kid anymore. We're practically adults, legally speaking, so why not invite him over on his day off?" Ayla and Mel sat at the kitchen table, sunlight streaming through the window, bathing their cozy nook in a soft, golden light. "I thought you wanted Hunter back home because he might mess something up."

Cradling the black box, I felt the mysterious palmetto paperweight buzz within. "This stupid paperweight zapped me when I stole it from Banning's desk. I don't know what kind of magic it's got or what kind of defenses it has. That's why I wanted Hunter back home."

"Wait, you swiped a paperweight?" Ami inquired.

Ayla's jaw dropped. "From a lawyer, no less?"

"While you were with Emma?" Ami shot a glance at Emma. "Doesn't she have to, like, arrest you or something?"

Emma stood by the kitchen table, her hand hovering over a porcelain dish filled with golden, crispy bacon. She looked up at the others with a mischievous twinkle in her eye, her lips curling into a playful smirk. "A stolen paperweight? I didn't see anyone nab a paperweight. No idea what you folks are on about." She blinked as she grabbed a piece of bacon and took a bite.

"Man, things sure are different around here," Ami remarked.

"You bet they are," Archie agreed, ruffling his

feathers and bobbing his owl head from the crystal chandelier hung from the ceiling. "Everyone's chowing down on bacon, yet nobody's offered me any. It's an outrage."

I rolled my eyes at Ami's concern, grabbed a slice of bacon, and held it out to Archie. "Please, I've stolen from more important people than Banning before. Let's focus on the task at hand, shall we?"

"Well, we need to figure out what the heck this thing does before we can do anything else," I said, setting the box on the table. "If I grab it and try to read it, it might fry my brain or something."

Mel leaned forward, his eyes bright with curiosity. "What if it's, like, a cursed object or something?"

I shot him a sideways glance, my tone dry. "Thanks for that brilliant contribution, Mel."

"Hey, don't discourage my boyfriend the way you discouraged your boyfriend," Ayla said with a wag of her finger. "I welcome his participation. Unlike the rest of you."

Ami raised an eyebrow. "You don't welcome our participation?" she asked.

"No, I meant that you discourage men."

"I do not. I have no opportunity to discourage men. I'd sell my potion collection for the opportunity to discourage men," Althea chimed in with a smirk. The crow, Lily, was perched on her shoulder, its black feathers shining in the light. She moved one arm to stroke her while the bird tucked her head into my sister's hair and nuzzled her. "Okay, maybe not my whole collection. I'm not that desperate."

"Speaking of your potions," I said, gesturing toward the black box, "I want to examine this palmetto thing in the potion room." I tapped the box for emphasis. "It's the most reinforced room in the entire house."

The potion room, with its sturdy walls and various protective enchantments, was an ideal space for handling the unknown—and dangerous—item we had acquired.

Borrowed.

Okay, I stole it.

Archie flew across the room and landed on my shoulder. As we made our way down the hallway and toward the potion room, my mind raced with the possibilities of what the palmetto paperweight could be. A cursed object? A powerful talisman?

"Is it crystal?" Althea asked, hurrying behind me.

"No, I think it's glass."

"Well, yes, I'm sure it is but is it crystal? Lead glass."

We opened the heavy door and stepped into the potion room. Shelves were lined with jars and vials, counters were covered in mysterious powders, and a few large cauldrons bubbled with unknown concoctions filled the room. Candles and wall sconces streamed light that illuminated the strange objects arranged on the tables and shelves. The air held a faint smell of sweet herbs.

"I'm not sure. You can—nope, uh uh." I shook my head, my gaze flitting to Emma as she hurried through the doorway. Lothian followed close behind her, his expression unreadable. "You'll have to wait outside."

"If this is about me being human? You can't be serious." Emma's tongue clicked between her teeth as she surveyed the room, disappointment etched on her face. "I didn't realize Arden House had a segregation problem."

I rolled my eyes. "This is about your safety."

She hitched her thumb toward Lothian, a defiant glint in her eye. "I have him."

Lothian chimed in with, "Yeah, she's got me."

Emma's confidence was impressive, but I couldn't risk anything happening to her, especially not in the potion room. "Sorry, Emma.

It's not about segregation. It's about safety. Lothian can't protect you from everything in here."

Althea's hands flew up, her elbows bent, and her palms open. "Look," she said, tilting her head. "You know how much I love to argue with Astra, but even I have to admit this isn't a safe place for either of you to be right now. You all got to go."

Emma crossed her arms and leaned against the door frame, a stubborn glint in her eye. "Fine. I'll wait outside. But if you need any help, don't hesitate to ask."

"We won't," I assured her.

"Uh-huh." With that, she turned and disappeared down the hallway, Lothian trailing behind her like a loyal dog...er, wolf.

* * *

ALTHEA and I opened the black box and placed the palmetto paperweight on the large black stone pedestal. It seemed to give off a faint luminous glow.

"It's lead glass," Althea said, nodding at the paperweight.

"What's the difference between lead glass and regular glass?" I asked her.

She launched into an explanation about lead glass, detailing how it was made differently than regular glass, with lead oxide mixed into the molten concoction of sand and other ingredients. "Lead has magical properties, too, making it a powerful focus for spells. That could be why the Palmetto Society chose these pieces for their members. Someone in the group knew what they were doing." She pointed out the paperweight had the Flower of Life etched into the bottom. "That's a sacred geometry background. The Flower of Life? That's a bit ambitious."

I stared at the paperweight. "What's the Flower of Life?"

"Really?" Archie asked and then nipped my ear. "You don't know?"

"Do you?"

"Of course. But you should let Althea tell you."

He didn't know.

Althea gave me a mischievous grin and propped her hands on her hips. "I don't think either one of you has a clue. Crack a book once in a while, will you? Anyway, the Flower of Life is a sacred geometric symbol that represents the cycle of life, death, and rebirth. It can be used in spells to bring about change and influence events."

"And what does it mean that it's in the background behind the tree?"

Althea gestured to the palmetto paperweight we had placed on the pedestal. "It's over the Flower of Life, so I think these people want to rule everyone. Based on these symbols, my guess would be that the Palmetto Society was formed with one goal: power and control. They want to be at the top of the food chain."

"Let's not forget your lead glass thing," Archie said. "In the world of alchemy, lead is linked to the planet Saturn and deemed the densest and most fundamental of the seven classic metals. Alchemists aimed to convert lead into gold. That has to mean something."

"In ancient times, lead was believed to have healing properties, and it was used as an ingredient in some medicinal remedies." Althea glanced toward the paperweight. "People also once believed that carrying a piece of lead or wearing lead amulets could protect them from evil spirits, negative energies, or curses. Which is ironic since it's deadly."

"So, putting together all this symbolic stuff, that paperweight symbolizes a change that gives —and protects—the Palmetto Society's power and money even though they're toxic?" I asked. "Am I getting this right?"

"Or," Archie quipped, "it could be a paperweight with a tree on it, and we should stop trying to find significance in every little thing."

"That zaps me with electricity when I try to hold it?"

Archie spread his wings in a defensive pose, the feathers on his neck bristling. "You act like that's a big deal! Zap it back already!" His beak snapped open and shut as if in disbelief. "You have the power of a star ping-ponging around your innards, and at most, that thing has the static from a nylon rug in a Colorado winter. Surprising? Sure. Painful? A little. Harmful?" He cocked his head to one side, an air of condescension in his voice. "Please."

Althea nodded in agreement with Archie. "He's right. You hardly ever use your star power, and it's a shame. I know how complicated it is to decide to unleash such immense power, but he's right. You should zap the thing."

"It's complicated, okay? I don't control my power. I unleash it, and it decides how to balance the justice scales, but not necessarily without hurting someone or accidentally destroying something."

Archie snorted. "How complicated can it be? You have the magical energy of a star coursing through your veins! You let it go, and it does what needs to be done. What could be so difficult about that?"

"I've gotta trust the power or the goddess who granted it," I explained. "And honestly, I don't trust either. I mean, I've met the whole Greek pantheon, even took a brief trip to the underworld's depths to fetch a hell-hound for Ayla—and drop off Mom and my boyfriend to their eternal doom. But Athena? Have I met her? Nope. My trust in her is lower than ever. If anything, it's hit rock bottom."

Althea glanced at me, remaining silent.

Archie leaned forward on my shoulder, his eyes growing wide.

"What?" I asked.

He hesitated before hopping off my shoulder, turning to face me, and gazing up at my face, his eyes blinking in quick, short flutters. He tilted his head ever so and gave me a condescending stare. "I only asked you to zap the glass doodad, Astra. No need to spend an entire potion room therapy session airing your divine grievances. We're all well aware of them by now."

Althea grimaced before nodding. "He's coming on strong, but he's got a point."

I could feel my irritation building up.

Sure, Archie and Althea had good intentions, but it seemed like they just couldn't fathom the depth of my reluctance or the possible fallout from tapping into my star power.

Mumbling to myself, I finally grabbed the paperweight, my annoyance driving my movements. "Stand back." Taking a deep breath, I homed in on my energy and unleashed a minor, measured burst.

The glass began to radiate a glow, vibrating so fiercely in my hand that I could no longer maintain my grip. As it slipped from my fingers, Althea's eyes grew wide in astonishment, gesturing for me to back away from the now unstable item as Archie flew to the other side of the room.

As we backed away, the paperweight shattered, sending shards of glass cascading in every direction. Blue-white energy ribbons and lightning-like bolts erupted from the shattered pieces, bouncing off the walls and leaving a bright, otherworldly pattern in their wake.

The lightning bolts dissipated and faded away, leaving only a few sparks before finally vanishing altogether. The walls were now free of any electric ribbons or lightning bolts, leaving behind a peaceful, calm silence in the room.

* * *

"WHAT THE HELL WAS THAT? Are you guys okay?"

Emma raced into the room, her face a mask of worry as she looked around. The next moment, Lothian was by her side, his gaze also sweeping across the scene before them.

"I guess this room's not completely soundproof." Althea moved toward them and assured them we were all fine. "It was sure something to see, though."

"Soundproof? The whole house vibrated!"

"I'm not surprised. It was awesome!" Archie nodded in agreement, his eyes shining with excitement as he recounted the events. "Beams and bolts and lightning! It was all glowy and bounced around like pinballs!"

"That bird is nuts," Althea said. "It was terrifying."

I cleared my throat before admitting that I had broken the paperweight. "I suppose that means I did, in actuality, steal the thing."

"Oh, please. You were never giving that thing

back to the crooked suit, and you know it." Emma's expression softened as she gave me an amused look before turning back to Althea. "So what happens now?"

"Now we fix it so Astra can read it without getting zapped." Althea swept the floor with a worn-oak broom that had seen better days, gathering up the hundreds of tiny slivers of glass in her dustpan. "And I think we should talk about Henry's confession last night while I put this back together." The tinkling noise of the broken glass echoed in our ears as she worked.

It was almost ten last night when Henry summoned the courage to tell us that he was in love with Scarlett Fields, his high school sweetheart. His words came out in a rush, like water breaking through a dam after years of pent-up pressure.

He explained their love was doomed from the start. Like some kind of berry farm Romeo and Juliet, their families interfered with their relationships, both believing a marriage between the two of them would threaten each family's legacy.

"Don't you think that could have something to do with this?" Althea carefully placed the broken pieces of glass onto the shining obsidian stand. "Especially if Barry Fields and Henry's father didn't want the kids to date or get married." She retrieved a velvet pouch from her pocket and poured out several silver-tinged droplets that glimmered in the candlelight. Methodically, she began to drip the drops onto the shards, her hand never trembling as she did so.

"Why would a high school relationship have anything to do with what's happening now?" Emma asked her. "He said he was still in love with her. We don't know how she feels about him."

"That, and his confession, makes me a bit more suspicious of Henry as a possible suspect." I leaned back, observing Althea as she pulled several pastel-hued droppers from her pocket. "Maybe he just brought that tire iron over here to make himself seem innocent. Maybe he killed her father because he couldn't live without her, and Mr. Misogyny said no again." I raised an eyebrow, allowing my imagination to run wild. "Maybe neither of these middle-aged people have gotten married because they're secretly seeing each other."

"Can you give me five minutes to put this paperweight back together before we spin off into another unsupported suspicion tangent?" Althea asked, her tone mildly exasperated.

"You wanted to talk about Henry's confession," I reminded her.

"Yeah, that was my fault," she said, an exasperated frown crossing her face. "I should have kept my mouth shut."

"I'm sorry. You're right. We need to stay on track."

Althea paused in her work and looked up at me, her expression softening. "It's okay, Astra. We're all just trying to figure this out." She stepped back, surveying her handiwork. "There. Good as new, just without all the magical defenses to fry your brain."

I reached out and took hold of the paperweight, determined to psychically uncover its memories. As my fingers touched it, I inhaled, letting my mind welcome the concealed part of the object, asking it to unveil itself.

The immediate connection catapulted me into a whirlwind of images, sounds, and emotions from the lawyer's office. Memory fragments flitted before me, crafting a rich tale of clients and dilemmas the paperweight had observed. Amid the sensory turmoil, I sought the most vital moment—the creation of the palmetto glass.

Calling up and isolating a specific memory proved—as I expected and as it always had been —a near-insurmountable challenge.

The tumultuous flurry of recollections started to calm.

I was just outside a clearing, though where I did not know. Trees rose up all around me, and their leaves rustled in the wind. Far above, stars twinkled, shedding a faint light on the scene below. In the middle of the clearing was a fire that blazed beneath a large palmetto tree.

It was then that I heard it—chanting.

Ex feminis viri, ex viris omnia.

Ex feminis viri, ex viris omnia.

The same thing Barry Fields had said before he was killed.

Chanting voices rumbled through the trees, a deep and formidable resonance that sent shivers down my spine. As I neared, I glimpsed silhouettes encircling a flickering campfire, their hooded figures leaning in sync toward a central spot.

Six.

There were six men.

Their faces were shadowed by their hoods, so it was impossible to tell who they were or what they were doing there in this dark corner of the woods in the middle of nowhere. The firelight shimmered across an array of palmetto paperweights that glittered on the ground in front of them like stars in the night sky.

Suddenly, they stopped chanting, and one by one, they took off their hoods.

They looked toward me and reached.

I screamed.

CHAPTER SIXTEEN

*M*y eyes snapped open, and I gasped for breath, my heart pounding against my ribcage. Sweat trickled down my forehead, and my hair clung to my damp skin. I felt a pair of strong arms wrapped around me. It was Lothian, his broad chest pressing against my back and his arms enfolding me in a protective embrace.

I turned my head slightly, and our eyes met.

"Are you all right?" he asked.

It took me a few moments to realize that I was back in the potion room and that the chanting and hooded figures had been nothing but a memory from the paperweight.

I shrugged off the werewolf's death grip,

trying to shake off the fear that had grabbed me along with the werewolf. "I'm fine. All of them looked at me, and it freaked me out." I looked around the room, trying to ground myself in the present.

Althea's brows knitted together, creating a deep frown that etched lines on her forehead. Her eyes narrowed, studying me intently. "What do you mean, they looked at you? You were just witnessing a memory. They couldn't see you."

"Yeah, well, they were staring at me," I replied. "All of them—six hooded figures around a fire chanting like they were in a cult. When they removed their hoods, they looked straight at me and reached out. Toward me. Like some creepy horror film zealots."

Lothian's expression softened slightly, and he reached out to place a comforting hand on my shoulder. "It's okay," he said, his voice gentle. "You're safe here, with us. We'll figure this out, I promise."

I shot Lothian a look, my eyebrows raised and lips pursed. "I know that, Lothian," I said, my tone laced with sarcasm. "This is my house and my own power, remember? I think I know about it better than you do."

Lothian's expression darkened, and his jaw clenched tightly.

Well, that struck a nerve.

I didn't care. I was tired of his constant hovering, his ridiculous attempts to protect me. I was a grown woman, capable of taking care of myself.

Lothian took a step closer, his eyes blazing with intensity. "Sorry," he said, his voice low. "I'm sorry I care about you. I apologize that I don't want anything to happen to you. Forgive me for having the audacity to be concerned."

"Passive aggressive much?" I shot back, my tone sharp. "I appreciate your concern, Lothian," I said, my fingers making air quotes around the word concern. "But I don't need you to be my protector. I can take care of myself."

"What am I missing here?" Althea asked.

Lothian's jaw clenched, his nostrils flaring with a hint of frustration. "I know you can take care of yourself," he said, his voice a low growl. "But that doesn't mean I can't worry about you. You screamed. You're one of the toughest women I know, and you screamed—that's a bit alarming. Sorry."

I held his gaze for a long moment, my anger slowly dissipating as I saw the genuine concern in his eyes. Lothian had a way of getting under my skin, of pushing all my buttons. "Right. Sorry."

Archie cocked his head to the side, his bright eyes fixed on me. "The two of you are adorable. He cares, she's fine, they're both sorry," he asked in a low, inquisitive tone. "Can we get on with this? What did you see before you hollered like a howler monkey at a banana buffet?"

I glared at him, took a deep breath, and recounted the details of my vision—the six hooded figures, the multiple palmetto paperweights, the chanting. Archie listened intently, his head bobbing up and down as I spoke.

Althea's eyes widened, and she let out a low whistle. "That's...interesting," she said with hesitation. "I wonder if there's a seventh person involved, carrying a seventh palmetto paperweight. That would explain why they were all looking at you. They weren't looking at you but at whoever held the paperweight." She pointed at the reconstituted lead glass paperweight.

Lothian frowned. "The leader, maybe?" he asked, turning to me. "Can you tell me again what you know about the men you saw?"

"I recognized Joe Banning, Scarlett's lawyer.

Brock Taylor was there. Deputy Abernathy." I frowned. "Talk about irony, by the way. The bonehead beating bushes to chase paranormals out of Central Florida is in a cult with magic paperweights? That's a plot twist."

"Okay, that's three," Althea said.

"Four. Barry Fields was there, too. There were two men I didn't recognize, and they sort of resembled each other. Maybe father and son?"

"Did you see Thomas Carmack at the berry farm the other day?"

I shook my head. "No, I was too busy hiding behind the generational jam shelves, and when I read the door, it only showed me the guy's back."

Althea nodded and quickly tapped her tablet, her fingers flying across the display. She had pulled up a series of images that filled the screen in seconds, showing a man posing with an older man.

"Here," she said, holding out the tablet to me. "Take a look at these."

"What am I looking at?" I asked.

Althea leaned closer, her eyes scanning the screen. "Thomas Carmack and his father, Gordon," she said, pointing to the younger Thomas as he stood before an older man with the same cold expression. "Were those two of the men you saw?"

"Yeah, that's them. The Carmacks were in the woods by the palmetto tree," I said, holding up the tablet for Althea to see. "But we still need to figure out the last two. And I heard them chanting that Latin phrase," I said. "Ex feminis viri, ex viris omnia. The same thing Barry Fields said before he died."

"You're kidding." Althea's eyes widened, and she looked at me sharply. "What does it mean?"

"It means those guys are misogynistic—"

"No, Astra, why were they chanting it."

Archie bobbed his head. "I need to find that palm tree—"

"Palmetto," Althea corrected the owl, her voice firm. "A palm is a type of tree or shrub with a tall, slender trunk and long, feathery leaves. But a palmetto is a palm tree native to the southeastern United States. It has a shorter trunk and fan-like leaves often used for thatching or weaving."

The owl's round, feathered head tilted to the side, and he looked at Althea. Then he blinked. He mockingly clicked his curved beak and said gruffly, "Of course. I do an immense amount of thatching and weaving." Archie then retorted sarcastically under his breath, rolling his eyes for good measure.

"You know, we'd get through all this much faster if you could speed up your sarcasm," I told him.

"What's next?" Lothian asked as he tried to steer us back on track. "We can't just sit here and wait for something else to happen."

"I agree we can't, but that's not what we've been doing, thank you." I glared. "I believe our top priority right now should be visiting Scarlett. We need to make sure she's safe and that she knows what's going on."

"Lily and I will help Archie try and find the palmetto clearing," Althea chimed in, her eyes bright with determination. "I'll also reach out to the pixies. They should know if there have been any fires near trees. That could be our best bet for discovering what's happening here."

Oh, awesome.

Yes, let's add pixies into this mess, too.

Lothian nodded. "Okay," he said. "Let's split up and get to work. We'll grab Emma and take her with us, then meet back here in a few hours and compare notes."

* * *

LOTHIAN EASED his tall frame into the driver's seat of my Jeep, his long legs folding gracefully as he settled behind the wheel. He adjusted the radio, fingers caressing the leather-wrapped wheel with a deft touch. Emma and I settled into the backseat.

"Wreck it, and we're going to have a problem," I told him. "I'm just saying."

Emma sighed.

Lothian's gaze in the rearview mirror flickered up to meet mine, his expression intense and focused. His hands tensed around the steering wheel and his jaw clenched. It was almost accusatory as if he was daring me to question him.

"I'm a werewolf, okay?" he said, his voice gruff.

"So?"

"I'm not going to wreck your Jeep."

I had no idea what Lothian being a werewolf had to do with his driving skills or my Jeep's immediate future, but he seemed to think that statement put the matter to rest.

"Werewolves are creatures of instinct," he explained as if he heard my thought. "We have heightened senses, reflexes, and strength. I can handle a car, Astra. Trust me."

"It's a Jeep," I said.

The engine roared to life as Lothian shifted into gear, his foot pressing down on the accelerator with a controlled force. We peeled away from the curb, the Jeep's tires screeching on the pavement.

"Slow down!"

"Will do," he replied. "And it's not like you need me to wreck your car to have a problem with me," Lothian muttered.

"What was that?" I snapped, my eyes narrowing as I glared at him in the mirror.

Lothian sighed deeply, his eyes flicking briefly to meet mine before returning to the road ahead. "Nothing," he muttered. "It's nothing."

I noticed Emma's movements out of the corner of my eye, her body language conveying a mix of curiosity, amusement, and concern. She shifted in her seat, her gaze darting between Lothian and me as if examining the heavy tension in the air. "Anything you two need the werewolf Queen Mother to get involved with?"

I let out a snort of laughter, unable to contain myself.

Lothian's eyes flicked up to meet Emma's in the rearview mirror. "I don't think involving the Queen Mother is necessary at this point," he said, his voice tinged with amusement. "But thanks for offering."

Emma nodded, a small smile playing at the corners of her lips. "Well, you never know," she said. "Sometimes it takes a little professional help to get to the bottom of things."

I leaned forward. "I don't think a detective is the professional help he needs."

Lothian let out a gruff chuckle at my words— but then he drew in a sharp breath as if startled, and muttered a curse.

A horn behind us honked.

And then another.

I turned to look out of the back just as he slammed on the brakes of my Jeep, the tires squealing as he swerved off to the side of the road. He jumped out without hesitation, sprinting toward the small wolf pup running down the street behind us.

"Oh my gods," I whispered, the blood draining from my face.

Cars honked in protest as the pup darted between them, desperately trying to catch up with us. "I don't believe it!" Emma shouted. "How did that kid get away from him this time?"

We tumbled out of the car after Lothian, and instinctive panic raced through me as my eyes landed on the chaotic scene before me. Hunter bounded toward us with a joyful enthusiasm that contrasted sharply with the danger he was in.

"I swear, I'm going to crate that kid," Emma told me as we raced into traffic.

Lothian was the first to reach him.

He approached the pup cautiously and reached out a hand, his movements slow and deliberate. Hunter sniffed at his fingers, his tail wagging happily as he licked at Lothian's skin. In the blink of an eye, the older werewolf scooped the wolf pup into his arms, Hunter's tiny body wriggling with excitement as the large man cradled him gently.

Emma sighed as Lothian placed the pup into her waiting arms. "Thank you."

"There's no need."

As we returned to the Jeep with the wolf pup cradled in Emma's arms, she leaned in close to the puppy, her voice filled with equal parts scolding and affection. "You're a naughty little thing, aren't you?" she said, her tone playful. "You're going to make Mommy put Daddy in the doghouse until you go to college, right? Yes, you are."

The wolf pup wiggled in her grasp, his tail

wagging furiously as he licked at her face with exuberant energy.

I slid into the front seat passenger side next to Lothian, a small gesture of trust after his death-defying rescue of Emma's mischievous ball of fluff. I couldn't help but feel a sense of gratitude toward him. His quick thinking and swift action reminded me of why I—vaguely—trusted him in the first place (even though he annoyed me.)

Well, that, and I was wearing black.

I loved the little fur ball but didn't want hair all over my outfit.

As we drove on, Lothian's acceleration was slower than it had been, his expression gentle as he periodically glanced at the werewolf puppy in Emma's arms. He seemed lost in thought, his eyes fixed on Hunter as if he were seeing something beyond the surface.

And, let's face it—he probably was.

His gentle demeanor starkly contrasted with the fierce intensity he displayed most of the time. It was almost as if he were a different person, capable of great strength as well as great tenderness.

For a moment, I found myself lost in contemplation, wondering about the complexities of the people around me and the hidden depths beneath the surface. It was a reminder that there was always more than meets the eye and that even the most unexpected people could surprise you.

* * *

WE PULLED up in front of the county jail, and my eyes were immediately drawn to the cold, unfeeling gaze of two guards as they walked through the parking lot. I couldn't help but feel a sense of unease as we made our way toward the entrance.

Lothian held the Jeep door open for Emma, his eyes meeting hers momentarily before he spoke. "I'll leave you the keys for the air conditioning," he said, gesturing toward the ignition. "You two stay here."

"You're awfully authoritative with my Jeep," I told him.

Lothian's lips twitched, the corner of his mouth turning up in a hint of a smirk. "You want to leave them out here in the heat?" he asked, keys held and dangling before me. "We could do that if you disagree with my planned course of action." Lothian's eyes held a steady gaze, a hint of challenge in his expression as he waited for my response.

I stared at him.

"Oh, man, you guys really are like an old married couple," Emma said, her expression serious as she took the keys from Lothian's outstretched hand. "Obviously, we'll stay out here, and thank you both for the air conditioning, and stop giving each other snark," she said, her eyes flicking toward me for a moment before returning to him. "Good luck."

Emma's words hit me like a bucket of cold water. I stared at her.

"Hey, I'm just saying," she said, shrugging. "You two bicker like an old married couple, but you obviously care about each other. It's kinda cute in a weird way. That I don't understand. Like, at all."

I was ready for this case to be over so the werewolves could return to their stone castle with their faux queen and adorable little furry enfant terrible.

I hated this case.

I hated this place.

And I hated his smug—

Well, that's not true, even though it rhymed.

I didn't hate Lothian.

But I wasn't thrilled being attached at the hip to the guy for the past few days.

The towering county monolith rose up from the ground like a great stone column with bars for accents and armed guards for decor. Its walls were made of concrete and steel, and the only sounds that echoed through the halls were the clanging of metal doors and the harsh commands of the guards.

As we made our way inside, the heavy metal doors clanging shut behind us, I couldn't help but cough. The air inside was thick with the scent of sweat and desperation, the sound of muffled voices and clanging bars echoing through the halls.

We made our way to the front desk, where the same gruff-looking guard sat perched on a high stool, his eyes scanning us with suspicion and disinterest. "What do you want?" he grunted, his tone bored.

"We're here to visit Scarlett Fields," I said, trying to keep my voice even.

The guard looked us up and down, his gaze lingering on Lothian for a moment longer than necessary. "ID," he said gruffly, holding out a clipboard.

As we handed over our identification and signed in, I frowned.

Something felt off.

I stepped closer to the guard's desk, eyes scanning the sign-in sheet for any inconsistencies or irregularities. But everything seemed to be in order, and the guard appeared to be going through the motions of his job without any cause for suspicion.

I shouldn't be uneasy. We knew so much more than we did last time. We learned about Brock's ties to Carmack, the secret Palmetto Society, and, most crucially, that Scarlett's lawyer did not have her best interest at heart.

And yet...I was uneasy.

And I didn't know why.

As he squinted at us, the guard's bushy brows twitched. He recited the directions slowly in a deep, bored voice, pointing down a hall I'd already been down when I visited Scarlett previously.

I couldn't shake the feeling of unease as we walked down the hallway toward the visiting area. Every step felt heavy, laden with an unspoken sense of danger.

My senses were on high alert, scanning our surroundings for any sign of trouble.

CHAPTER SEVENTEEN

*D*espite my spidey sense popping off like a group of hyperactive toddlers on a sugar high, nothing stood out as being out of the ordinary.

Well, out of the ordinary for a jail, anyway.

As we entered, the room was filled with the cacophony of families visiting inmates—a jumble of voices that mixed relief, laughter, and tears. Lothian and I weaved through the crowd until I spotted Scarlett perched on a hard plastic chair at a small table in the corner, her eyes fixed on us.

"Scarlett," I said, my voice warm. "It's good to see you again."

Scarlett leaped from her chair, her face lighting up as we approached. But before she could get too carried away, the guard ordered her to sit back down. She obeyed, though the gratitude in her voice was unmistakable. "Astra! I didn't expect you to come back," she said.

I couldn't help but wonder what kind of disappointment Scarlett had endured making her assume we would leave her in jail without a second thought.

"We've been working hard to get to the bottom of this," I said. "We've uncovered some information, and I can fill you in on the details. But the biggest problem is that we're almost certain your lawyer is involved in this framing."

"More than positive," Lothian said, certainty in his voice.

Scarlett's eyes widened in astonishment, and she leaned in closer, her gaze locked on me. "What do you mean?" she asked, her voice tense.

I took a deep breath and launched into a detailed account of what we had discovered so far, deliberately omitting how we'd come across the information. I revealed that it appeared her lawyer had been in communication with Brock Taylor and that we suspected he might be working against Scarlett's best interests. I explained Brock's ties to Thomas Carmack and the existence of the secretive Palmetto Society.

Scarlett's expression grew increasingly troubled as I spoke, her eyes widening with each new detail. When I finished, she exhaled a heavy sigh, her shoulders drooping under the weight of defeat.

"I can't believe it," Scarlett exclaimed, her voice full of despair. "I trusted him. And nothing you said makes sense considering what Mr. Banning told me. He said I'd be released once they arrested Henry Johnson for the murder. And you said Henry had the murder weapon, so that fits."

"Henry Johnson?" Lothian leaned in, his eyes fixed on Scarlett. "Your lawyer told you that Henry Johnson killed your father?"

Scarlett nodded. "He told me yesterday afternoon when he called that they found the murder weapon on Henry's farm, with his fingerprints all over it. But I can't believe Henry could do something like that—we dated in high school long ago. Did you know that?"

"It seems like everybody knows where this tire iron is before the tire iron knows where it is," I remarked dryly. No one knew but us and Henry Johnson. Unless Banning had a time machine, he couldn't know the tire iron was on Johnson's property.

Well, and whoever planted it.

"How did you find this lawyer, Scarlett? Who recommended him to you?" Lothian asked, his tone measured and low.

"Brock. Why?"

I shared a concerned glance with Lothian. The more we uncovered, the murkier the situation seemed to become.

"Brock," I muttered, barely audible. "He's involved in everything."

Scarlett nodded. "He told me Joe Banning was a close friend of my father's and had provided legal counsel for the farm." She sounded uncertain. "I trusted him. Brock, I mean. It didn't help his job if the farm fell apart because my dad was dead and I was in jail, right?" She paused, frowning. "But you're saying he might have recommended a lawyer to me who wanted me in trouble, and if that's true, can I trust Brock?"

I certainly wouldn't.

Leaning in close, Lothian fixed his eyes on Scarlett. "We wouldn't recommend trusting him," he said firmly. "But ultimately, the decision is yours. What do you think based on what we've told you and what he's told you?"

Scarlett hesitated for a moment before answering. "I don't know," she said finally.

"When he visited me here, he swore to me that he'd ensure that Dad's legacy was protected and that Carmack would never get a hold of our farm."

I frowned, my mind racing. "When did he say that?" I asked.

"When he brought the papers for me to sign the farm over to him temporarily," Scarlett replied, her voice heavy with emotion. "You know, while I'm stuck in here."

Lothian looked at the farmer's daughter. He seemed to be searching for a hidden meaning that could explain Scarlett's trust in Brock despite all the problems they'd had between them.

"Why did you trust him, Scarlett?" Lothian asked, his voice low and serious.

Because drowning men grab any lifeline.

Drowning women, too.

After a long pause, Scarlett finally looked up at him, her eyes full of emotion. "I don't know," she said, her voice trembling with uncertainty. "He just...seemed like he wanted to help me. He knew I'd inherited the farm before I even knew my dad left it to me, and he'd been there for ten years. I know he's kind of a jerk, but he cared about it, too."

"Wait a minute." I turned to Lothian, my eyes

narrowed. "Brock knew that she inherited the farm?" I asked, my voice tinged with disbelief.

Lothian pressed his palm flat on the table as if bracing himself for impact.

Scarlett nodded. "Yes, he did," she said. "He said he would protect it for me until all this stuff about my dad got worked out. He knew I'd never hurt my father."

"Astra's a bit surprised because we overheard Thomas Carmack—we think—and Brock Taylor speaking the day after your father passed away. Neither of them," he said, "seemed to think you owned the farm."

I frowned, my mind racing. "We've been thinking there were two wills all this time because that's what we were told," I said.

"But only one person told us that." Lothian looked at me. "Henry Johnson told us there was a second will leaving the farm to Brock Taylor," he said. "Not Taylor. Not anyone other than Henry Johnson."

* * *

As we stepped into the county jail lobby, the feeling that something was off still nagged at me. I couldn't shake the sensation that the air was thick with secrets, as though the atmosphere held whispered conversations and furtive glances. I was missing something. I knew it.

What was I missing?

Lothian nudged me gently and gestured toward the guard's station. "We need to pick up our identifications from there," he reminded me. "Then we can go talk outside."

A sudden realization dawned on me, and I snapped my fingers. "Bingo."

"What?" he said, a look of confusion on his face. "What do you mean?"

"That's it," I said, my gut instinct telling me we were on the verge of uncovering something crucial to our investigation. "That's what's different." I pulled him away from the guard's counter and lowered my voice. "We didn't even have to show our IDs the first time we were here. Or sign in. They just waved us in."

Lothian's eyebrows knitted together as he considered my words. "You're right," he admitted. "I don't know how I missed that."

Because I'm better at this than you, I thought to myself.

Silently, he turned his attention to the guard, observing the check in process with keen interest. "That's one," he noted as a woman handed over her identification.

"And two," I whispered a few minutes later as an elderly man followed suit.

"Three," he whispered a few minutes later.

A warm, deep voice interrupted our counting. "Ya'll really gonna just stand there and count visitors?" A kindly-looking dark-skinned man inquired from his seat in the waiting room. His eyes sparkled with amusement as he continued, "Because if you're waiting to see someone get in without handing over their ID, you'll be waiting a while. That's something everyone has to do."

Lothian stood tall, an air of confidence surrounding him, but a closer look revealed a subtle tension in his frame at the older man's interruption—like a coiled spring, ready to leap into action at a moment's notice.

As I tried to decide how to react, my phone, nestled against my hip, buzzed insistently, pulling my attention away from the eavesdropper and the check in process. I glanced at the screen, seeing Althea's name flashing in bold letters. I swiped to answer the call.

"Astra, I've got news," Althea's voice crackled through the line, her excitement palpable. "I didn't want to send it in a text in case you get arrested or something."

The way this was going?

It was a legitimate concern.

Lothian leaned in closer.

"We're both here," I told Althea, my voice hushed. "Who is it?"

"The prints belong to someone named Roland Ball," Althea announced triumphantly. "Now, here's the wild part—he's a correction officer working at the jail you're visiting and previously worked for Carmack Aggro Holdings. It's probably a little more than a coincidence."

Just a little.

"We didn't see a deputy on Henry's property. We saw a uniformed correction officer," I guessed, my voice barely audible. "That uniformed officer."

My gaze drifted across the room to where Roland Ball stood, my eyes settling on the broad-shouldered man as he stood at his post, a look of concentration etched onto his features. The queue snaked around his booth, each waiting their turn to be inspected and cleared for entry.

"I think he's technically a deputy, but you're right. He told us he had a friend at Scarlett's farm," Lothian reminded me, his voice tinged with urgency. "Do you remember that toxic rant he went on about her when we visited the first time?"

Officer Ball's words had been laced with venom. At the time, it had struck me as petty small-town gossip—and entirely unprofessional.

But now, with Althea's revelation?

The pieces were starting to form a more sinister picture.

"Excuse me." The elderly black man leaned toward us, his face breaking into a warm smile, his eyes sparkling with kindness. Despite his slender frame, he exuded a remarkable sense of poise and grace as he sat on the hard plastic chair. "I didn't mean to overhear your conversation, but I couldn't help myself."

Uh-huh.

"You do know that young man at the counter used to have a crush on Miss Scarlett back when she was just a girl, don't you?" His tranquil expression conveyed a profound sense of calm. "I remember it like it was yesterday. He was sweet on her, always stealing glances and trying to get her attention. But he was too shy to make a move."

"How do you know that?" I asked the man.

"I spent my life teaching in this town. Andre

Dupont at your service," he said, holding his hand out. "I came here from Haiti with nothing in my pockets but lint, and this great county let me teach its next generation. Isn't that amazing?"

Though I wanted to be wary and distrustful of the man, I simply couldn't bring myself to do so. "Nice to meet you, Mr. Dupont."

"Oh, please. You call me Andre," he replied, shaking my hand with a firm grip. His watery eyes narrowed as he studied me closely. "I know all the stories everyone would love this town to forget, and I have a memory like an iron trap." He tilted his head. "You're Jason's girl, aren't you?"

The retired teacher's mention of my deceased ex-boyfriend hit me like a physical blow, the pain still raw but somewhat dulled with time. "Yes, I was," I said, my voice trembling as I swallowed the lump in my throat. "Did you know Jason?"

"I did, yes. Jason was a wonderful young man," Andre replied, his smile softening with fondness. "I remember him well." The kindly man's expression darkened as his gaze flicked toward Roland. "Mr. Ball, on the other hand, is not such a lovely young man," Andre continued, his tone tinged with disappointment. "I wish I could say otherwise. He had so much potential, but he let his anger and bitterness consume him."

"Why do you say that, Mr. Dupont?" Lothian asked.

"Andre, big man. I told you, call me Andre. You call me Mr. Dupont, and I feel like I should start teaching you Algebra." He leaned in, his voice hushed but filled with conviction. "Roland might have been a good boy, grown up to be a good man if he hadn't met that no-good Tommy Carmack. Take a young man like that from a poor neighborhood, show him speedboats and vacations in Paris, and tell him he can never have them on his own?" The man's eyes widened as if newly shocked by the decades-old observation. "Tommy turned that boy greedy. Greedy and mean."

Lothian and I exchanged a glance, taking in Andre's words.

The revelation added another layer to the already complex picture of the men in the berry farming community and further entangled the intricate web of relationships and motives surrounding Scarlett's case.

"But loyal?" Lothian asked Andre, his eyebrows raised in curiosity.

"Loyal?" I raised an eyebrow.

"You know what I mean, don't you, big man?" The elderly man nodded, his face solemn. "Oh, yes, Tommy Carmack never met a more loyal soldier than poor Roland." He gestured to the officer leaning against the counter with a scowl on his face. "He followed Tommy around like a puppy, always trying to do whatever Tommy said and sometimes going above and beyond what was asked of him. The Carmacks gave him a job at the berry plant for years. Did you know that?"

May all the gods bless all the old people, I thought to myself.

They had a lifetime of gossip stored up and were always excited to find someone to listen to it.

I scrutinized Roland, wondering what compelled him to abandon such a seemingly dedicated role. He appeared sullen and aloof, his gaze unfocused and distant. It was clear that he lacked any real passion for his work.

Andre seemed to read my thoughts. "I never quite understood why Roland left his position at Carmack's farm a year ago and came here," he mused. "But I suppose he needed a change. Sometimes change can be good, but other times it's just a way of avoiding something." The elderly man let out a wistful sigh, his eyes wandering toward the window.

His voice tinged with a hint of contemplation,

Lothian said, "And other times, it's simply a matter of putting all the pieces in place for a very long game." The werewolf directed my attention to a directory on the wall and motioned for me to examine it more closely. "Take a look at room forty-two," he said.

I followed his gaze and scanned the directory, my eyes landing on the entry for room forty-two.

County Evidence.

* * *

EMMA's BROW furrowed in confusion as she played with the wolf puppy in the back seat of the Jeep. "So, let me get this straight," she said, her voice tinged with skepticism. "You think the Carmacks had Roland leave their employ and come to work here just so he could steal the tire iron from evidence, plant it at Henry's, and let Brock Taylor into the visiting area without there being any record?"

I could see the gears turning in Emma's head as she tried to make sense of our latest theory. It was a convoluted one, to be sure, but it was the only one that made sense, given the evidence we had gathered so far.

I nodded, my expression serious. "It's a

possibility," I said. "The Carmacks have a reputation for being ruthless, and they'll stop at nothing to get what they want."

"And why did he let you two in without signing in?" she asked.

I shrugged. "No idea."

Emma let out a sigh and shook her head. "I can't believe we're caught up in this mess," she muttered, scratching the puppy behind his ears. "All I wanted to do was help a friend. Okay, I also wanted to solve a simple mystery to stretch my legs and feel like I was back in the game, but mostly to help a friend. Now we're knee-deep in a conspiracy. I don't like conspiracies. They're very messy." She looked at me. "Another question. What is the deal with these stupid paperweights, then? Is the fact that these guys are in a cult just a coincidence?"

As if on cue, my phone buzzed once more. I switched it to speaker mode.

"So, I think the ball is rolling downhill and picking up speed. Roland's name led to many other records, including his purchase of an ancient Roman lead coin at an auction in Sarasota a couple of years ago. It was notable for two reasons. He bid five million dollars for one, and he only makes fifty thousand a year working for the Carmacks," Althea reported breathlessly. "Where did he get the money?"

"He was a cover for the real buyer," Emma murmured, her voice low and thoughtful.

"Oh, hey, Emma! Yeah, that's what I figured," Althea agreed.

"What was the other thing?" I asked.

"There's a phrase on the coin. I'll give you three guesses what that phrase is," Althea teased. "First two don't count."

"Ex feminis viri, ex viris omnia," Emma, Lothian, and I said simultaneously, our voices mingling in a chorus of recognition.

Hunter barked.

"See, you didn't need three guesses," Althea said, her voice laced with amusement. "I heard a bark. Is that Hunter?"

"Long story," Emma said.

"Not really." I reached out and pet the wolf, feeling the softness of his fur under my fingers. "Eddie and Emma have a smart kid that wants to be with Mom."

The puppy barked again.

The revelation about the mysterious coin and its connection to the enigmatic phrase only deepened the intrigue surrounding Scarlett's predicament.

But I felt we were close.

I knew we were close.

"Oh, and Archie wanted me to let you know he found the clearing with the palmetto tree. It looks like someone's there," Althea added. "He left Lily there to watch the guy."

We were on the brink of unraveling the tangled web of deceit.

I could feel it, like electricity in the air, almost palpable.

But before tackling this latest lead, we had a small but essential task to complete–taking the baby werewolf home.

CHAPTER EIGHTEEN

As Lothian steered the Jeep into the driveway of Arden House, the golden rays of the setting sun cast a warm glow on the colonial. Shadows stretched before us, long fingers of darkness reaching for the building that held so many magical secrets.

Before I could even unbuckle my seatbelt, Eddie appeared from around the corner of the house. His usually confident stride seemed somewhat hesitant, his shoulders slumped as if weighed down by his inability to contain the newest member of his pack.

"Oh, dear," Emma sighed.

Lothian and I had braced ourselves for the

potential storm that would be Emma's reaction to Eddie letting Hunter, the baby wolf, escape yet again.

But instead, her eyes softened with sympathy as she approached him, a knowing look in her eyes.

When they were a few feet apart, she bent down and gently released the tiny, silver-furred creature from her arms. His delicate paws touched the well-worn brick path lined with fragrant gardenias. "Hunter's fine. It's okay," she told Eddie, a reassurance that lingered in the humid Central Florida air. "We got him."

"Emma, I'm—"

"Don't apologize." She cut him off with a tender smile, dimples showing as she tilted her head. "We're in this together. We're only going to solve this together. I'm sorry it took me a while to realize that."

Eddie's expression was a mixture of sheepishness and mild embarrassment. He ran his fingers through his disheveled hair, his dark eyes revealing vulnerability beneath furrowed brows. "You and I will figure this out, Emma. I promise."

"Absolutely." Emma's confident statement was accompanied by a determined nod, her shoulders squared and her posture exuding assurance.

Hunter, the ever-energetic pup, sprinted toward Eddie with uncontainable enthusiasm, his paws scuffling against the gravel drive. His pointed ears perked up as he yipped and wagged his bushy tail wildly. The wolf's sheer delight seemed contagious, and the scent of blooming jasmine in the surrounding gardens filled the air, adding to the sense of warmth and comfort.

Eddie crouched down to meet the excited pup, one hand reaching out to ruffle the soft fur on Hunter's head. "I hope so because, at the moment, I feel like he's smarter than us."

So did I, but I didn't say anything.

We climbed the steps to Arden House's imposing front entrance. The great oak door, adorned with intricate carvings, creaked open, and Hunter's tiny wolf claws skittered across the polished wooden floor, his boundless energy undaunted by the house's dignified ambiance.

Althea's voice rang out from the depths of the house, breaking the silence. "You guys! Come on, I've got something to show you!" Her tone was a mix of excitement and urgency.

As we approached the kitchen, the aroma of something delicious wafted through the air, a blend of aromatic spices and fresh herbs that made my stomach rumble in anticipation.

The kitchen was warm and inviting, with a large, well-worn wooden table taking center stage. Aunt Gwennie always kept the copper pots and pans hung from the ceiling shined so they reflected the flickering light of candles and cast a cozy glow over the room. "I have some pasta," she said, gesturing. "You can eat it before you take off again."

"Thanks."

"While we're waiting, come here." Althea leaned over the table, a mischievous glint in her eyes as she beckoned us to gather around her laptop. "That?" she said, pointing. "Is the Cursing Coin of Actaeus."

"The what of the who now?" I asked.

"The Cursing Coin of Actaeus. It's also known as Actaeus' Infandum Numisma," Althea said. "And it's got a heck of a story."

As we gathered around the table, Althea started the tale.

In the dark days of ancient Rome, there lived a man named Actaeus, a skilled blacksmith and devout worshipper of Mars, the god of war. Actaeus had a deep hatred for women, stemming from his mother's abandonment as a child and his failed relationships with the women he encountered throughout his life.

"So, an ancient Roman incel?" Emma asked.

"Yeah, kind of. Anyway, Actaeus got it in his head that he needed to create this charm to protect guys from women and give them some kind of power against them."

Ayla, who'd joined us, rolled her eyes.

Legend had it that Actaeus approached the Oracle of Delphi and requested the secret to create a powerful charm that could fulfill his desires. Sensing his malicious intentions, the Oracle denied his request, warning him that pursuing such a path would only lead to his ruin. However, Actaeus, undeterred, embarked on a quest to learn the secrets of the gods themselves.

"Oh, that's going to go well," Emma said sarcastically.

"Right? Eventually, he came across this cult worshipping an ancient goddess named Cybele. The cult's leader offered to teach him how to make the charm in exchange for his soul. Actaeus, being super obsessed with this whole thing, agreed."

"Why do people agree to things like that?" I muttered under my breath.

Emma furrowed her brow and glanced at me, her eyes filled with doubt. "Why?" she asked. "You can't really take someone's soul, right?"

The four of us turned to look at Emma, our faces mixed with amusement and disbelief. Despite all we had seen and experienced, she maintained a subtle sense of naivete that was both endearing and frustrating.

Althea let out a small chuckle, her eyes twinkling behind her glasses. "You really are something, Emma," she said, shaking her head in disbelief. "We need to get you a paranormal handbook."

Ayla grinned, her dimples deepening as she leaned back in her chair. "Don't tease her. She'll search for this mythical paranormal handbook like a caffeine-deprived college student looking for the last Red Bull on exam day."

Emma blinked. "Wait—there's no handbook?"

Ami poked her head in from the other room. "What's going on?" she asked.

"Your sisters are teasing me that there's a book that explains all of you and all of this. "Okay, never mind," Emma said, surrendering. "Souls can be snatched, stolen, and bartered. I stand corrected."

"I'd just like to point out I teased no one," I said.

"Of course not. You'd need a sense of humor for that," Ayla told me.

I glared.

"Can I go on?" Althea asked.

We nodded, and she did.

Actaeus poured his hatred and bitterness into the coin, Althea went on, inscribing it with the symbols of Mars and Cybele and the quote we're now all so familiar with. When the coin was completed, it was said to radiate a sinister energy that could corrupt men's hearts and repel women's influence.

"People called it 'Actaeus' Infandum Numisma' or the Cursing Coin of Actaeus," Althea said. "It started causing all sorts of problems."

As news of the Cursing Coin spread, many men sought to possess it, believing it would grant them power and control over women. The coin changed hands numerous times, sowing discord and strife wherever it went. Families were torn apart, marriages crumbled, and women were subjugated in the name of the coin's dark power.

Eventually, the Cursing Coin found its way back to Rome, where it caught the attention of Emperor Marcus Aurelius. Recognizing the danger posed by the coin, the emperor ordered it to be destroyed. "He had it thrown into this pit that was supposed to be a gateway to the underworld and sealed it away for good," Althea finished.

"Obviously," Aunt Gwennie said as she brought pasta bowls, "that pit wasn't deep enough."

* * *

"The lead glass paperweights," I said once we finished eating, my voice taking on a thoughtful tone as I recalled the magically repellent object we'd encountered earlier. The buzzy, electrified defense of the paperweight had left a lasting impression in my mind. "They took the cursed coin and made lead glass paperweights out of it so all their crazy tree cult members could get a bit of the misogynist magic."

"That's what I think, too," Althea said.

"That's a tiny amount of lead, though, right? How much lead do you need to make lead glass?" Emma asked, her fingers tapping rhythmically against the wooden table that anchored the cozy kitchen. "More than a coin's worth, right?"

"The amount of lead required to make lead glass depends on the desired optical properties, as well as other characteristics of the glass," Althea explained, her tone patient and knowledgeable. "So, they could use as much or as little as they wanted."

Ayla frowned and pushed a strand of hair away from her face as she leaned back in her chair. "Let's back up. Who's in this cult group again?"

I closed my eyes briefly, picturing the eerie gathering beneath the fanned fronds of the palmetto tree. "I saw Gordon and Thomas Carmack, Brock Taylor, Barry Fields, and Joe Banning," I said, ticking them off on my fingers as I spoke, my gaze drifting from one concerned face to another around the table.

"That's only five. I thought there were six," Ayla said.

Lothian, seated beside Ayla, counted the names off on his fingers, his lips moving silently as he did the math. "Well, seven total, but we're not sure who one of them is since Astra didn't get a look at their face," he said. "But you did say Deputy Abernathy was in your vision before, Astra."

I nodded. "Yes, that's right. Deputy Abernathy was there, too. He was standing off to the side."

So who's the seventh person with the seventh

paperweight?" Ayla asked, her voice a mixture of curiosity and apprehension. "It has to be someone with fingerprints on the tire iron, right?" She turned to me. "You saw that it was the murder weapon for sure, didn't you?"

"I did."

Ayla looked at Althea. "Whose prints did you find?"

"Henry Johnson, Scarlett, and Roland Ball."

"It has to be Henry Johnson, right?" Ayla said, her voice tinged with conviction. "His fingerprints were on the tire iron, he's a berry farm owner, and it seems like this is some kind of berry-farm-owning cult thing. Scarlett also broke up with him in high school, so he killed her father and framed her. He must be the seventh berry-growing woman-hater."

"Oh, I can't believe that it's Henry," Emma told Ayla, her eyes filled with doubt. "He got us onto the Fields farm so we could poke around, and Astra said she basically watched some kind of cult meeting out at that palmetto tree in her vision. Would you really hate the guy you're in a cult with?"

"What do you mean?" Eddie asked.

"Henry and Brock openly despised one another," I told him. "Like, you could practically feel the 'I hate you' energy coming off both of them."

"Barry was in the cult, too," I said, "and someone whacked him with a tire iron. Maybe liking one another isn't a prerequisite to whatever they're trying to do."

"Or maybe they just kept up appearances to keep people from suspecting anything strange was happening? Hiding the truth because they were both in on it?" Lothian said. "I'm kind of with Emma on this, though. I just don't think Henry has it in him. He seems like a genuinely good guy."

"You guys are making a lot of judgments based on your feelings," Ayla said.

"What about Roland Ball?" I asked, furrowing my brows as the memory of our first encounter with him came to the forefront of my mind. I leaned forward in my seat, resting my elbows on the table. "His fingerprints were on the tire iron, too, right? When I first met him, he had burns on his fingers." I held my hand up, mimicking the location of the burns on Roland's fingers. "He told me he worked with glass at a Renaissance fair—but it's May. The Florida Renaissance Festival is in March, not May."

"February and March," Eddie corrected, glancing at the others. "But you're right."

Emma looked at him, her eyes narrowing with curiosity. "And how would you know?" she asked, tilting her head to one side.

Eddie's cheeks reddened ever so slightly, but he said nothing, choosing instead to stare intently at a small crack in the wooden tabletop.

Emma's expression shifted from amusement to understanding as she connected the dots. "He must have made the lead glass paperweights for the cult."

Lothian, seated to my right, absently twisted his silver ring as he considered the new information. "If he was responsible for making the paperweights, it's possible he's deeply involved in the cult." He shifted on his chair, the old wooden legs creaking beneath him. "I didn't give him much thought because everyone else in the group are men of power and influence, and Roland Ball is anything but a man of power or influence."

"Oh, come on!" Althea, sitting beside Emma, snorted and rolled her eyes. "When have men of power and influence ever done their own dirty work?" she asked, her voice dripping with sarcasm.

Ami had been shuffling her tarot cards as she listened to us discuss the information we had. She flipped over a card, revealing the Five of Swords.

"What does that mean?" Emma asked, her eyes darting between the card and Ami's face.

Ami chewed her lower lip as she formulated her response. "So, if you asked which tarot card could represent a group conspiracy, the Five of Swords would be a good one to look at."

Althea leaned in, her dark eyes reflecting the dim light. "Basically, it's all about betrayal, conflict, and doing whatever it takes to come out on top, even if it hurts others."

"The card shows a person holding three swords and two more lying on the ground behind them, which suggests a win through unfair means or at the expense of others." She looked up. "Maybe it's more than one person."

The scent of pasta sauce no longer felt comforting.

* * *

HENRY JOHNSON.

Roland Ball.

One of those men held the tire iron that whacked poor Barry Fields...

Well, maybe not poor Barry Fields.

The guy was a member of a cult that hated women.

I stood on the back porch, my hands gripping the wooden railing and eyes scanning the sky, the colors of dusk bleeding together into a magnificent yet unsettling canvas. The large backyard seemed to stretch endlessly, the shadows of the trees growing long and eerie as the sun dipped below the horizon.

Archie should have returned from the palmetto tree an hour ago, and I was growing annoyed at his late arrival. We couldn't leave for the clearing until the birds returned and showed us where it was, and I was growing restless and impatient to get a move on.

"I'll nuke you some bacon if you get your tail feathers back here. Come on, dude," I whispered. I shifted my weight from one foot to the other, my impatience evident in every movement.

The back door creaked open, and the sound of footsteps broke the quiet of the evening. "He's not back?" Lothian asked me.

I shook my head, my eyes still trained on the darkening sky. "No, not yet."

As Lothian came to stand beside me, I caught a whiff of his intoxicating scent—that signature blend of sandalwood and cedar that made my stomach flutter with a feeling I was not willing to examine, much less name. I tried to focus on the task, but the warmth radiating from his body was impossible to ignore.

I shifted my body, moving away from him so I could no longer feel him near me. The tension between us was low-key but noticeable, and I couldn't help but feel a sense of unease as I looked away.

"Is that him?" he asked, pointing as he shifted closer to me.

You've got to be kidding me.

"No," I told him. "That's a hawk."

The werewolf stood close enough once more that the slightest movement from either of us caused his arm to brush against mine. I shook my head to clear my thoughts, forcing myself to concentrate on the matter at hand.

The owl.

I'm looking for the stupid owl.

"Astra—"

The back door swung open again, revealing Emma and Eddie, their animated conversation spilling out onto the porch and cutting off whatever the werewolf had been about to say. Hunter, their energetic wolf puppy son, burst from behind them, wagging his tail and perking up his ears while barking excitedly.

Lothian and I exchanged a look.

His eyes showed he was aware of the unfinished moment, and my face probably showed that I was glad the werewolf queen and her alpha-ish consort had stopped him from saying whatever he was about to say.

Lothian cleared his throat and shifted his weight, turning away from me to engage Eddie in conversation. Their voices melded together, a low murmur that I couldn't quite decipher as they walked toward the edge of the porch, leaving me with Emma and Hunter.

My best friend stepped closer, her brow furrowed with curiosity as she studied my face. "So, did anything happen between you and Lothian?" she asked, her voice barely above a whisper. "Because judging by your face, if I had to put money down, I'd bet a twenty that it did."

I felt my cheeks grow warm, and I crossed my arms defensively, trying to regain my composure. "Why would you even ask that? No, nothing happened," I replied, perhaps a bit too quickly and far too defensively. "We were just, you know, waiting for Archie. And talking. That's all."

Emma's eyes twinkled with mischief as she

tilted her head, unconvinced by my hurried response. "Uh-huh, sure," she teased, a knowing smile tugging at the corners of her lips.

"Oh, just shut up, will you?" I rolled my eyes, trying to brush off her playful insinuations. "Seriously, Emma, we were just discussing the case," I insisted.

Though it felt like a lie. I couldn't deny the lingering feeling that something more had been in the air. To myself, I mean. I couldn't deny it to myself.

I'd deny it to Emma until her puppy went to grad school.

She let the matter drop, though her grin suggested she didn't quite believe me.

Together, we joined Lothian and Eddie, our conversation shifting back to the investigation as we waited for Archie's return, the unspoken connection between Lothian and me simmering just below the surface in furtive glances across the patio.

A sudden, piercing screech tore through the air, shattering the relative calm of the evening. I jerked my head upward, my heart pounding as my gaze locked onto Archie, perched on a nearby tree. His eyes were wide, and his feathers seemed to bristle with frustration.

"We have to go! We have to go!" he shrieked, his voice urgent and panicked, cutting through the night like a knife.

"Why?" I called.

"They got him!"

CHAPTER NINETEEN

When Archie told me that Henry Johnson was tied up under a palmetto tree in the center of the clearing he'd been sent to find, everything started to fall into place.

I remembered Virgie, the old woman we met at the berry farm, and her description of Thomas Carmack's suspicious actions before the murder. He asked endless questions about the farm's operations—why?

I recalled Brock's sarcastic smirk as he joked with Carmack about Henry possibly murdering Barry Fields for the coveted strawberry jam recipe. I remembered that he had visited Scarlett

Fields in jail and somehow convinced her to sign over control of her father's farm to him.

The cursed coin that Roland Ball had purchased with Carmack's money...

Abernathy's sudden appearance on the scene...

They all took on new significance in light of these revelations.

"It's the Carmacks," I blurted out, quickly making my way to the driver's seat of the Jeep. Emma and Lothian were right behind, jumping into the vehicle. Lothian settled in the back while Emma sat in the passenger seat beside me.

"Okay, tell me more," Emma said.

We drove down a narrow dirt road, the trees on either side looming over us like gnarled fingers clawing at the Jeep. The dim light from the dashboard cast eerie shadows, making the interior feel spooky and unsettling. It was as if we were racing against time, and the atmosphere only added to the sense of urgency.

I explained to Emma and Lothian, gripping the steering wheel tightly as I spoke. "Henry was the only one who mentioned two wills," I said. "He had talked to Joe before he talked to us and even mentioned the name of Scarlett's lawyer, whom he planned to see after us. That must be where he got the information, even though it turned out to be wrong."

Emma's voice was calm and steady as she eyed Archie's direction and instructed us to turn right. As we drove, the scent of damp earth and the distant hum of insects filled the night air. "Okay, but why? And why the county and Abernathy? What do they have to do with this?"

"Aside from the obvious cult member thing?" I asked.

"The guilty parties needed someone on the inside, a law enforcement officer they could manipulate," Lothian said thoughtfully. "By bringing in Abernathy, they hoped to control the investigation and prevent themselves from getting caught."

I tapped my fingers on the steering wheel, thinking out loud. "You know, if Abernathy can produce some evidence of the occult in this murder—or blame it on the occult—he will have free rein to chase all of us all over the county."

Lothian nodded thoughtfully, his eyes reflecting the faint glow of the dashboard lights. "Yeah, true. And that coin didn't just repel women, remember? It protected the men from the women."

Emma's expression grew tense as she

informed us that Archie had stopped. "He's just sitting in that tree up there," she said. "We must be close."

She scanned the darkness for any sign of danger as Lothian, and I exchanged glances.

* * *

WE CLIMBED out of the Jeep, our footsteps muffled by the damp earth. The night air hung heavy with anticipation, the scent of pine and wet foliage filling our lungs. As we crested a hill, we saw a soft light flickering through the branches of the trees ahead, casting an otherworldly glow on the scene before us.

"Is that a fire?" I whispered, pointing to the flickering light.

Emma nodded slowly, her eyes narrowing as she studied the flickering light. The tension in her stance was palpable, her muscles coiled like a spring ready to leap into action. Her fingers brushed against the small of her back, where she kept her gun hidden from view.

"What do you think they're doing?" I asked in a hushed voice.

"I don't know," Emma replied, her voice

equally quiet. "But whatever it is, we need to be prepared for anything."

As we crept closer, a peculiar warble reverberated through the air. It sounded almost like someone had taken Latin lessons from a yeti, the off-key chanting echoing out of place in the Florida wilderness. The voices seemed to weave together, forming a sinister tapestry of discordant sound that hung in the air like a bad karaoke performance in a dive bar.

"What the heck is that?" Lothian whispered, his voice tense with apprehension.

"Why is chanting always a big thing with cults?" Emma asked, her eyes scanning the area for any sign of movement. "It's enough to make your ears bleed."

Suddenly, we heard Henry yelling at them, his voice filled with defiance and desperation. "You won't get away with this! You people are crazy!"

Emma's eyes darted with determination as she assessed the best course of action. I could see the gears turning in her mind, her expression shifting from concern to resolve as she mentally pieced together a plan.

Emma motioned for Lothian and me to circle around the clearing, flanking the dissonant cult members from both sides. With practiced stealth, we each moved through the underbrush in opposite directions, our senses heightened in anticipation.

I finally caught a glimpse of them through the brush. There were no robes this time. They stood in a semicircle surrounding a bound Henry Johnson seated with his back against the palmetto. A large bonfire blazed behind them, casting flickering shadows on their forms.

I could see the sweat on Henry's forehead, his eyes darting from side to side as he struggled against his bonds. "Let me go!"

In a sudden burst of movement, Emma stepped out from behind the trees, her gun raised and aimed at the berry-planting woman-hating paperweight-carrying cult members.

"Stop right there!" she shouted, her voice strong and commanding. "You're all under arrest for kidnapping and conspiracy!"

The cult members whirled around, their faces twisted in anger and surprise. There seemed to be a tense standoff for a moment as Emma held her ground, her eyes locked on the men before her.

Then, to my surprise, one of them began to laugh.

Deputy Abernathy.

He greeted Emma's arrival with a wry smirk,

twirling his lead glass paperweight in his right hand. The fiery light from the flames made the glass glimmer as he leveled a steady stare at her. "Of all people, it had to be you," he muttered, his tone amused. "Don't worry, gentlemen. Not only is she only a woman, she's not even a detective."

I really wanted to punch that guy in the face.

More than once.

"This is a real gun, Deputy," Emma shot back, her voice steady despite the tension in the air. "I don't think bullets have a gender identity or a gender preference. They'll tear holes in anyone."

I scanned the clearing and took in the familiar and expected faces of Detective Abernathy, Brock Taylor, Joe Banning, and the Carmacks—Senior and Junior. They stood there, dressed inconspicuously in street clothes, each holding their paperweights with a menacing grip.

"What the hell are you doing here?" Abernathy demanded. His eyes were narrowed in suspicion.

"What does it look like?" I whispered to Archie.

He hooted softly in response.

Man, these guys were boneheads.

"I'm here to take you and your fellow cult members into custody. And, you know, I could ask you the same thing," Emma replied, calm and level, "but I already know the answer. You're all in on this, aren't you? The kidnapping, the cult, everything."

I could see the fear in Abernathy's eyes, the uncertainty that belied his confident words. He reached toward his empty holster for reassurance, but his hand closed on nothing. There was no gun there.

"Forget something?" Emma asked him, eyebrow raised.

The lawyer, however, had no such lack of confidence. "You're way out of your depth, kid. This is bigger than you. Besides, there's six of us," Joe Banning pointed out, "and only one of you."

I couldn't help but smirk at the realization that Abernathy was unarmed.

And that they thought Emma would show up alone.

Emma didn't flinch, a slight smirk playing at the corners of her lips. "You guys are a little too confident in your size," she said, her tone light and mocking. "You shouldn't go bragging about it —people that brag generally can't back it up."

Ouch.

Their statement wasn't entirely accurate, though. Joe had said there were six of them, but I could only see five men, or six if you included

Henry Johnson. I doubted that Joe was counting him.

I looked around nervously, scanning the trees for any sign of movement.

Nothing.

"Roland Ball must be lurking around here somewhere," I whispered to Archie, my voice low and urgent. "Do you see anything? You're better at seeing in the dark than I am."

Without hesitation, the owl spread his wings and took flight. "I'll go look."

I watched as he soared into the night sky, his sleek form disappearing into the darkness.

Back in the clearing, the powerful, arrogant men that formed the Palmetto Society exchanged uneasy glances, unsure how to respond to Emma's confident taunts. They seemed to expect her, being a woman and all, to cower in fear when faced with their superior numbers and blistering wit.

But she stood her ground, her gun still trained on the cult members.

This seemed to baffle them.

Carmack Junior stepped forward, his expression twisted with anger. "You think you're so tough, don't you? Let's see how tough you are when we're through with you." He brandished the paperweight like a loaded gun, shaking it menacingly at Emma. "Do you know who we are?"

Emma didn't flinch, her eyes narrowing in defiance. "Berry farmers with delusions of grandeur?" she asked. "Pathetic, cowardly men who think they can get away with murder?"

"Thomas, are you planning to argue with her all night, or will you do something?" Scarlett's crooked lawyer, Joe Banning, asked the apparent leader.

Thomas Carmack glared at him, his face twisted in anger. "Shut up, Banning."

But Banning wasn't intimidated. He stepped forward, his face set in a determined expression. "I thought you said those paperweights were our protection against people like her."

People like her.

You know.

Women.

"In case you've forgotten, this jerk stole my paperweight from my desk." Banning gave Henry a shove with his foot, still bound and helpless. "I don't have one, so do something!"

I could feel the tension in the air as the two men glared at each other, the sound of the nearby bonfire filling the clearing. But then, suddenly, the crackling of the flames was drowned out by a low, menacing growl that seemed to come from somewhere deep in the darkness.

"What the hell was that?" Brock Taylor's voice was filled with fear as he spoke up. "I never signed up for this, Carmack," he said, his words trembling. "I thought we were just taking advantage of a business opportunity that came our way after Scarlett's father died."

Thomas Carmack glared at him, his expression cold and hard. "You knew what you were getting into, Taylor," he said sharply. "Don't act like you're innocent now."

"Scarlett didn't kill her father, you fool!" Henry interjected.

"He's right," Emma said firmly, her eyes fixed on Brock Taylor. "We have Roland Ball's fingerprints on the tire iron that killed Barry Fields, and we caught him on surveillance cameras dropping it on Henry's farm to frame him."

Brock looked visibly shaken by that news, his face pale with shock. "I...I had no idea," he stammered. "I was just doing what I was told." He turned toward Thomas. "I always wondered why you gave that guy a paperweight. Abernathy, too. We all ran farms, Banning represented farms, but they had nothing to do with farming. Nothing. You acted like they belonged here—"

Thomas Carmack confronted Brock with a scowl, his eyes filled with anger. "You knew what we were doing the whole time," he said sharply. "Don't play dumb like you had no idea. What did you think we were doing out here?"

Brock's eyes flicked nervously between him and the rest of the group. "I...I didn't know it would go this far," he stammered. "I thought we were just making some easy cash and complaining about women, that's all."

But Thomas wasn't buying it.

He turned to his father with a look of disgust. "Can you believe this guy, Dad?" he said. "He's just trying to save his own skin."

Gordon Carmack's eyes swept over the clearing, his face devoid of emotion. I realized that he hadn't said a word since we arrived, and the silence from the elder Carmack was starting to feel unnerving. I couldn't help but wonder what was going through his mind.

"Dad?" Thomas Carmack's voice was concerned as he looked at his father. "Do you have anything to say?"

More silence.

Joe Banning cleared his throat, breaking the

tension in the air. "Mr. Carmack, do you have anything to add?" he asked, his voice surprisingly calm.

But Gordon Carmack's response was anything but calm. "Why hasn't anyone shot her? Shoot her," he said quietly, his eyes fixed on Emma.

"A police officer? Are you crazy?" Brock asked.

For a moment, no one moved. The air was thick with tension, the silence of the night broken only by the crackling of the nearby bonfire.

Gordon Carmack's eyes flickered toward Abernathy, but he remained silent. It was like he was a statue, observing the clearing from a distance. The longer he stood there, the more uncomfortable I felt.

"You're a deputy—you don't have a gun? Shoot her."

"Thomas told us not to bring them out here," Abernathy responded. "He said just bring the paperweights. That's all the protection we would need."

Boneheads.

Absolute boneheads.

"I'm surprised this plan worked at all," he remarked. "Given that you lot are utterly witless."

* * *

GORDON CARMACK CAST AN INTIMIDATING FIGURE, towering over the small group with his imposing frame. His angular features were sharp and unyielding, giving him a fierce and commanding presence. Despite his quiet demeanor, an aura of danger and unpredictability surrounded him as if he were constantly assessing the situation and calculating his next move.

"How did you find us?" Gordon asked Emma.

"What does it matter?" Emma asked him, her voice laced with a hint of anger. "The fact is, I know you and your son are behind all of this. And now that we have the evidence, there's no way you're getting away with it."

"You have no evidence." Gordon's expression remained unreadable as he contemplated her response. The crackling of the fire and the rustling of the palm trees around us was the only sound that broke the silence. "Who helped you?"

"This isn't a postmortem on my handling of the case," Emma told him. She gestured toward Henry, who was still bound to the palmetto tree. "And he's my evidence. Someone needs to let him go. Now."

Gordon's eyes flickered toward Henry, who

sat bound on the ground nearby. "You may have found us," he said, "but the game is far from over."

"Oh, yeah, Mr. Bond Villain? What now?" Emma remained unflappable, her determination unwavering.

Gordon's lips twisted into a cold smile. "There is only one of you, and most of us are protected against you because you're a woman."

"You're bulletproof, are you?"

"Maybe."

Emma's grip on her gun tightened. "I have a bunch of bullets in this gun," she said, her voice cold and unwavering. "And I'm willing to bet they'll disagree with you."

"You may have bullets," he said, his voice low and dangerous, "but we have other means of protection. Magical means. Otherworldly means. Something far more powerful and ancient than anything you could possibly have."

A low, guttural snarling noise cut through the tense standoff in response to the Palmetto Society member's uneducated assumption. The sound was coming from the darkness beyond the clearing, and I knew all too well what—and who —was making it.

Archie flew onto my shoulder and whispered urgently in my ear. I nodded.

Taking a deep breath, I stepped out into the clearing, Archie perched menacingly on my shoulder. "She's not alone," I said, my voice clear and confident.

Thomas Carmack glared at me, his eyes burning with anger. "Who's this?" he demanded.

Before I could respond, Gordon Carmack interrupted, muttering under his breath, "Witless. And yet, even with these idiots, I set up a murder, a frame-up, and another frame-up in only six months! Before the end of the night, this idiot," he pointed to Henry, "will be dead. So will both of you!"

Brock Taylor looked stricken. "I didn't sign up for murder! I won't be a part of it any longer."

"It's over, done," Gordon declared, his eyes flickering between us, his expression turning dark and dangerous. "In one week, I will own every berry on every berry farm in Central Florida for a pittance! Sad? I'll be the happiest, richest man in Central Florida!"

"And that was what I needed." Emma stepped forward, her gun trained on Gordon, and flashed the wire she was wearing under her shirt. "You're finished, Gordon. We have everything we need to bring you and your associates to justice," she said. "And we are, by the way, in Forkbridge. Just in case anyone is curious about any jurisdictional issues. So, yes, friends—you are all going to jail."

"Arrest us for what?" Brock Taylor asked. "I didn't know about any murder!"

I pointed at Henry Johnson, still tied to the palmetto tree.

"Oh," he said. "Right. Him."

Yep.

Him.

Gordon struggled to mentally process the sudden change of events, and his face twisted with rage as he lunged forward, determined to take down Emma before she could take him down.

But she was prepared.

Emma's extensive training and lightning-fast reflexes shone through as she nimbly sidestepped his assault and floored him with a single well-timed strike.

A hulking wolf materialized from the shadows a second later, its penetrating gaze fixed on Gordon. It stood its ground, snarling menacingly over him as if to warn him not to get up again.

Feeling the sudden shift in their fortunes and hearing the distant wail of sirens, Gordon's lackeys quickly surrendered with their hands raised high. From his kneeling position, Joe

Banning blurted, "I want my lawyer to talk to the prosecutor. I'm ready to cut a deal!" He pointed an accusing finger at Gordon. "It was all him! All him!"

"Hey, have you seen Roland Ball?" Emma asked, glancing around the clearing.

In an instant, Archie took off toward a nearby tree where Roland was hiding, his wings flapping with impressive force as he went into attack mode. Roland raised his arm, bracing himself for the worst as he aimed it toward the feathered predator charging at him. But it was too late. With talons outstretched and razor-sharp, Archie swooped down upon Roland, striking him.

I winced at the sound of Roland's arm snapping under the impact.

"Found him!" Emma said, gesturing toward the fallen suspect.

CHAPTER TWENTY

"When exactly did you get in touch with the chief?"

Emma leaned back in her chair at Arden House, her eyes twinkling as she filled us in on what we didn't know. "Well, I've been updating him all along, but when the situation started to heat up, he insisted on being in the loop. That's why I wore the wire. He began mobilizing a response team when he heard we'd located Henry and that the guy was tied to a tree."

Her voice was tinged with a hint of pride, and I couldn't help but notice the faintest smile play on her lips. Emma loved Hunter and being a mother more than anything—but solving a case for her came a wicked close second.

We were seated back in the cozy living room of Arden House, the flickering glow of the summer fireplace (it's a witch thing) casting dancing shadows on the walls. The scent of burning wood and a hint of lavender from a nearby candle filled the air, creating an atmosphere of warmth and comfort–starkly contrasting the almost disastrous events we'd just experienced.

"Here you go, Astra." I glanced up to see Lothian offering me a steaming mug, his eyes filled with concern. "If it's too sweet, just let me know, and I'll whip up a new one for you."

I nodded my thanks, accepted the tea, and tried not to watch the tall, dark, and handsome werewolf as he retreated to the kitchen. "So, did we ever figure out why those goons had no firearms?" I asked Emma. "It seems a bit shortsighted to kidnap someone, whisk them away to their secret cult hideout, and then fail to secure the place properly."

Emma pursed her lips thoughtfully before responding. "It does seem like a wild oversight, doesn't it? Here's the thing about criminals in a conspiracy—they don't exactly trust one another. Young Carmack feared someone might betray him or his father, seeing they had the most to gain. So, he instituted a strict no gun policy. That's why Ball was in the tree. He was a lookout —if he saw something, he was supposed to shout."

I chuckled. "I guess we weren't something."

"Or he was just terrible at his job."

"You did have a gun. He was probably just hoping you wouldn't see him."

Ayla, her eyes wide with curiosity, slid onto the couch next to Emma and asked, "So, they all did it? They conspired to kill Barry Fields and frame Scarlett and Henry just to get their hands on those berry farms?" She furrowed her brow, shaking her head. "I mean, I love berries, but seriously? What's the big deal with berries?"

Emma chuckled softly and leaned in, explaining, "It wasn't about the berries, Ayla. It was all about profit and control. The Carmacks wanted to dominate the market, Joe Banning aspired to rule an empire, and as for Abernathy— who knows what he wanted out of all this. Honestly, I don't get the guy."

Althea strolled into the living room, her dark hair messy, and said, "Abernathy's just a witch hunter. Do you know what most witch hunters really want? Magic. Only a handful really want us destroyed. Most just want what we have." She shrugged. "He's no different. I bet they dangled those magical paperweights before him, and he couldn't resist the temptation."

Ayla frowned. "We still have to deal with those, by the way."

"I'll get them before I go to bed." I casually flicked my fingers, generating sparks of lightning that danced at their tips. "No problem."

"Why didn't you just zap everyone in the clearing and let the goddess's justice sort them out?" my sister asked me, her curiosity apparent.

"It was Emma's case," I explained. "We handle it the way she wants to."

Ayla seemed to understand my reasoning. "Makes sense. We've all got our own ways of dealing with things, right?"

"Exactly," I agreed. "And respecting each other's methods is part of what makes teamwork so strong."

Eddie walked into the room, cradling a now-normal baby Hunter in his arms (thanks to one of Althea's meticulously brewed potions that prevented the little minx from shifting.) He glanced at Emma with a warm smile. "Are you almost ready? I think we should probably get Hunter home. He's bound to sleep for a few days after all the excitement."

Emma looked up at him and smiled. "Just about, yes."

I took a sip of my tea, feeling the warmth spread through my body as I watched Eddie and Emma exchange a look that spoke volumes. It was a look of love, gratitude, and of relief. The kind of look you only shared with someone who had been through the worst with you and came out on the other side.

As they stood up to leave, I couldn't help but feel a pang of envy.

Oh, don't get me wrong.

Honestly, I was happy for them, but it was hard not to feel jealous. I had just gotten comfortable with the idea of being in love and of being in a relationship when my mother's petty jealousies killed my boyfriend. I'd never been in love before that, not really. I had had my fair share of flings and one-night stands, but nothing had ever felt real.

Jason felt real.

Lothian caught my eye from the kitchen as he handed Aunt Gwennie a dish towel, and for a moment, my heart skipped a beat. But as soon as that feeling crossed my awareness, I felt a strange sensation creeping up my spine. It was like a sixth sense warning me that something was off.

I closed my eyes.

It's just adrenaline, I told myself. The criminals we nabbed weren't the most well-prepared, but things could have gone wrong.

It was still stressful.

Just adrenaline.

I opened my eyes to see that Lothian had returned from the kitchen and was now standing opposite me. He looked down, watching me intently, his eyes glowing in the dim light. I felt a flutter in my chest but quickly dismissed it.

Lingering effects of adrenaline.

You can blame a lot on adrenaline.

It's very versatile.

"You okay, Astra?" he asked, his voice deep and soothing.

I nodded. "Yeah, I'm fine. Thanks for the tea."

Lothian smiled.

I felt a sense of relief wash over me. Henry was safe, the bad guys had been caught, and Hunter was back to being a regular old baby. In a few minutes, I would explode the ineffectual misogynist paperweights like a cheated-on ex-girlfriend in a rage room.

It was almost too good to be true.

Lothian leaned down. "Goodnight, then."

I gave him a small smile. "Night."

* * *

THE DESTRUCTION of the magical paperweights turned out to be surprisingly anticlimactic. I should have guessed it would be, though—I'd wondered why, considering the palmetto people were a cult with magical paperweights, they hadn't attacked us with said magical paperweights.

As it turns out, magic born from hate has a significant limitation: it can only generate more hate. That need to feed hatred?

Yeah, it rendered the stupid paperweights incapable of much else.

A not so subtle reminder that love and unity were far more powerful forces.

Archie, perched by the attic window, announced his intentions with a soft hoot. "I'm going to hunt." His large owl eyes studied me as I changed into shorts and a t-shirt. "You okay? You seem a little off."

Brushing off his concern with a casual smile, I replied, "I'm fine."

The room, illuminated by the silvery moonlight streaming through the open window, seemed filled with our unspoken emotions. Despite my reassurance, Archie's expression still showed concern. It was a testament to our bond, a connection that transcended the boundaries of the natural and supernatural worlds.

That, and the bird was just really nosy.

Archie's feathery head bobbed up and down. "So, you don't want to talk about it?" He tilted his head slightly. "Right. I get it. You never want to discuss your feelings, which, if I'm being honest, is one of the things I like about you."

I raised an eyebrow in mock surprise, pulling back the covers and sliding into bed. "Oh? There's something you like about me?" I teased. "Well, that's news. Archie, I'm genuinely touched."

"See?" He ruffled his feathers, feigning annoyance. "This is precisely why I don't say anything." With a graceful leap, the owl launched himself through the open window, his feathers eerily silent as he took flight. The night swallowed him, his majestic form disappearing into the moonlit shadows.

"Good luck," I called after him, turning off the lamp beside my bed.

An otherworldly blue glow emanated from my mirror, almost instantaneously casting its ethereal light across the room. Sighing, I rolled over, curious to see whether it was Jason, my mother, or some other spirit from the underworld reaching out to me just as I was about to drift off to sleep.

"I'm sorry to bother you so late, but this is the first time you've been free since you met Mr. Dupont," he said. "I'm glad he was helpful with your case."

I sat up in bed, my gaze fixed on the mirror. "Well, it wasn't really a case. The goddess didn't assign it to me, and I don't work for the police department. Emma's on vacation, too, so it was just to help her friend. Did you see Hunter?"

Jason's smile was warm and genuine. "I did. He's a beautiful baby."

"He is. As a baby and a wolf."

A comfortable silence settled between us before Jason spoke again. "I know you've been struggling lately, Astra. With your mother's actions and my death. There's something I've been meaning to talk to you about."

I hesitated for a moment before speaking. "I'm doing better. I still feel guilty. It's true. Your mom wasn't wrong that I'm a little responsible for what happened to you."

He dismissed my concerns with a wave. "That's nonsense, and you know it. I know you're tired, so I'll get right to the point. I've been keeping an eye on you, Astra," he said, his voice low and serious. "I've noticed that you've been getting closer to Lothian."

I frowned, feeling a twinge of annoyance. "No, I haven't."

"You're going to lie to a dead man?" he asked, his tone amused. "As if I haven't been through enough?"

In the soft blue light of the mirror's glow, I found myself torn between the past and the present and wondering what the future held. It was difficult to admit the thought had crossed my mind at all to Jason, whose presence in my life still held a unique place in my heart. Caught off guard by his lighthearted approach to the topic, I couldn't help but smile sheepishly.

"Okay, let me try this another way," he said. Standing straight and tall, he looked me in the eyes and said, "Astra, I will always love you, but we exist in different realities now. This doesn't change how I feel about you, and I will always be there for you if you need me—but I've met someone down here. I'd like to pursue it."

I braced myself for anger or jealousy to wash over me.

But it didn't.

Instead, I felt relieved.

"That's wonderful, Jason. I'm happy for you. For both of you."

And I really was.

He offered a half-grin in response. "Your mother most certainly isn't happy for me, but Persephone is having a ball keeping her in check."

I couldn't help but chuckle at the image of my mother being managed by the formidable queen of the underworld. Life, or rather the afterlife, was full of surprises, and as Jason's words sank in, I realized that maybe it was time for both of us to embrace new beginnings.

We chatted for half an hour about his new love interest. She sounded perfect for him. She was a teacher, too—which didn't surprise me.

As we talked, a sense of peace settled over me.

It was comforting to know that even though I had lost Jason in the physical world, he and I could still connect. And it was reassuring to hear him encourage me to move forward with my own life and to know he was doing so as well.

Eventually, our conversation ended naturally, and Jason bid me goodnight. The blue glow of the mirror faded, leaving me in darkness again.

But this time, the darkness felt less overwhelming, and I drifted off to sleep with a sense of contentment.

* * *

THE NEXT MORNING, I awoke feeling refreshed and ready to face the day. I got dressed and headed downstairs to the kitchen, where Althea and Ayla were sitting at the table, sipping coffee and chatting animatedly.

"Good morning, lazybones," Althea greeted me with a grin as I walked in. "Did you have a good night's sleep?"

"I did, actually," I replied, grabbing a mug and pouring some coffee. "I had a nice chat with Jason last night."

"Oh?" Ayla said, her interest piqued. "What did he say?"

"He just wanted to check in and see how things were going," I said with a shrug. "And he's met someone down there, so he's moving on."

Althea gave me a sympathetic smile. "That must be hard for you, Astra."

I shook my head. "Actually, it's not. I'm happy for him. And for myself, too."

"Why's that?" Ayla asked.

"Because it made me realize it's time for both of us to move on," I said.

Althea and Ayla looked at me in surprise.

"Move on from what, exactly?" Althea asked.

"From the past," I replied, sipping my coffee. "From all the hurt, guilt, and regrets. From a sense of obligation to something that doesn't exist anymore. I think it's time for us to start fresh and embrace new beginnings."

Ami, who had just walked in, grinned at my words. "I like the sound of that!"

"Me too," Althea said, her expression softening.

"I believe I can sign up for that," Aunt Gwennie added as she placed toast and a bowl of jam on the table. "It's about time for all of us, I think. By the way, that jam?" My aunt's face looked confused. "Emma called this morning and said that you would want to try some of it—she gave me a recipe and told me someone had been murdered over it?"

"It was an old family recipe from a hundred years ago. The Fields ancestors stole it from the Johnson ancestors, or so the story goes. We thought it might be part of the case, but it wasn't," I said, grabbing a piece of toast and a spoonful of jam. I took a bite. "I don't get it. It just tastes like jam."

"It is just jam," Aunt Gwennie answered.

"Any special ingredients?" Althea asked.

"I made it with strawberries, sugar, lemon

334 | LEANNE LEEDS

juice, and pectin. It was quite simple to make. It called for a dash of cinnamon, which was a little unusual. But it's just jam—nothing to kill anyone over, certainly."

"Unbelievable," I said with a sigh.

Aunt Gwennie rolled her eyes. "What wouldn't people kill over these days?" she asked, exasperated. "I swear, I don't know what the world is coming to. In my day—"

"It's still your day, Aunt Gwennie," Althea said, offering a reassuring smile. "And people will kill each other over anything, it seems."

"Well, hopefully not for a few days," Ayla said. "I'd like to see my boyfriend."

Ami raised an eyebrow, teasing, "Oh, so Mel's a boyfriend now?"

"Shut up."

As we finished our coffee and headed out to start the day, I couldn't help but feel grateful for the strong, magical bonds of sisterhood and family that held us together.

I looked around the table and smiled.

Aunt Gwennie, with her sharp wit and old-fashioned sensibilities; Althea, the book-learned brainiac from Smartron; Ayla, with her youthful enthusiasm and drive; and Ami, the level-headed voice of reason. Together, we were a formidable team, each with our own unique strengths.

And with each step forward, we left the shadows of the past behind, embracing the future and the untold possibilities it held.

* * *

THANK YOU FOR READING!

I hope you enjoyed Owl Berry Mysterious. Please think about leaving a review! Astra, Archie and the whole Arden family continue their adventures in Book 13, Of Owl the Nerve.

KEEP UP WITH LEANNE LEEDS

Thanks so much for reading! I hope you liked it! Want to keep up with me?

Visit leanneleeds.com to:

Find all my books…

Sign up for my newsletter…

Like me on Facebook…

Follow me on Twitter…

Follow me on Instagram…

Thanks again for reading!

Leanne Leeds

FIND A TYPO? LET US KNOW!

Typos happen. It's sad, but true.

Though we go over the manuscript multiple times, have editors, have beta readers, and advance readers it's inevitable that determined typos and mistakes sometimes find their way into a published book.

Did you find one? If you did, think about reporting it on leanneleeds.com so we can get it corrected.

ARTIFICIAL INTELLIGENCE STATEMENT

Portions of this book were created with the assistance of AI tools used for editing, proofreading, and refining the text. However, the ideas, storyline, characters, and overall creative vision remain my own original work.

While some aspects of the cover image were generated using AI tools, it was done so under my creative direction and curation.

I want to acknowledge the use of these technologies as part of my creative process, while affirming that the essence of this work comes from my own imagination and effort.

Leanne Leeds

www.ingramcontent.com/pod-product-compliance
Lightning Source LLC
Chambersburg PA
CBHW021443240626
47153CB00001B/266